LYNTON
AND
THE LADYSMITH PHANTOM

By

J. Wayne Frye

#15 in the Lynton Series

Notice:
This book is written in Canadian English, so
teachers should alert their students
to the differences in spellings.

Lynton and the Ladysmith Phantom

TO:
Nicolas and Joni – old and
dear friends from long ago.
And
Lynn and Rodney: They were rarely seen over the
years, but each visit by them to my château was
treasured and savoured.

Also, as always, to my muse:
Lynton Globa Viñas – the dynamic dynamo.

Catalogue Number: 971362-2020
ISBN: 978-1-928183-44-0

FIRESIDE BOOKS - CANADIAN DIVISION
Part of the Peninsula Publishing Consortium

J. Wayne Frye

Wayne Frye's Lynton series started with the heroine when she was in the Philippines, then followed her to South Africa and now she has arrived in Canada, where she is ready to settle down to a quiet life in the small town of Ladysmith, British Columbia on lovely, pristine Vancouver Island, but things are about to go terribly awry. As a renowned demon hunter, when strange occurrences start plaguing a friend, her special skills are sorely needed. This may be the most horrifying Lynton adventure yet, as she tries to solve a mystery that has perplexed people for over one hundred years.

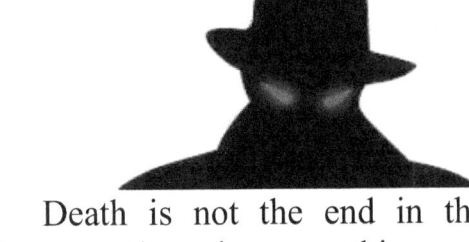

Death is not the end in this thriller, because there is some thing, some entity that wants to do harm, needs to do harm, feeds on harm and relishes the fear it instils. This is a demon similar to one which Lynton encountered before, but this one is more menacingly sinister because of its seemingly benign appearance.

The Real Lynton Viñas

J. Wayne Frye

Lynton and the Ladysmith Phantom

<u>Table of Contents</u>

Lynton and the Ladysmith Phantom

About the Author

Wayne Frye's *Aaron Adams* mysteries, *Chablis Louise Chavez* thrillers, *Girl* books and *Lynton* adventures titillate the brains of those who enjoy tantalizing tales of mystery. Growing up in the small town of Asheboro, North Carolina, he wrote his first novel at 15, but waited over twenty years before finally submitting it to a publisher. His life, like the heroes he writes about, has been filled with adventure and excitement. He has been a college hockey coach, professor, and at one time the youngest university president in the USA. Called a marketing genius by the *Los Angeles Times*, he has been a promotional consultant to hockey teams and motion picture companies. Additionally, he has been cited for his work with inner-city gangs in Los Angeles. A proud Canadian, he lives in Ladysmith, British Columbia on beautiful Vancouver Island.

Some of the 49 books by J. Wayne Frye

Hockey Mania and the Mystery of Nancy Running Elk
Something Evil in the Darkness at Hopkins House
White Meteors and the Ghost of Sue Ann McGee
How Hockey Saved a Jew From the Holocaust
The Girl Who Said Goodbye for the Last Time
The Girl Who Motivated Murder Most Foul
The Girl Who Stirred up the Whirlwind
The Girl Who Rode into a Storm
Fall From Apocalypse
Armageddon Now
Sammy Sasquatch and the Sts'ailes Star
Worth Part 1: Roaring Through Life Like a Comet in the Midnight Sky
Worth Part 2: The Night of Thunder Road
When Jesus Came to Jersey as the Son of Thunder
When Jesus Came to Canada to Lead an Indigenous Rebellion
When Jesus Came to the Black Hills to do the Ghost Dance
Lynton Curls Her Hair
Lynton Walks on Water
Lynton and the Vampire at Tagaytay Manor
Lynton Buys a Cell-Phone and Hears the Voice of Doom
Lynton Viñas and Beowulf Perez in the Taal Inferno
Lynton and the Ghosts in the Mansion on Balete Drive
Lynton Viñas: Shadow in the Darkness
Lynton's South African Adventure
Lynton, the Karoo Vampire and the Jewels of Omar Bin Abi
Lynton and the Haunting of the HMS Wind Dancer
Lynton and the Stellenbosch Terror
Lynton and the Cape Town Ghost
Chablis: Avenging Angel for the Forgotten
The Rectifier: Dance of Death in the Darkness of Retribution
Chablis and the Terrorist Who Resurrected the Spirit of Che Guevara
Pursuit

J. Wayne Frye

Prologue
A Warning

A shadow in black without a name,
Did an icy-cold heart it have? Who to blame?

Are you dead and for others want the same?
Oh, the black shadow perilously came.

She had a bearing of confidence as she strolled
off the plane, walking toward immigration with
her usual quiet air of fortitude apparent to all. Her
assured manner was not born of arrogance, not
born of her incredible beauty, not in any way born
of her superior intelligence, but it was merely an
outward manifestation shaped from many years of
having to fight for survival in an extremely cruel

environment that was based on that old adage that greed was an enviable trait, because it was the grease that oiled the capitalistic machinery that grinds up workers to make the privileged richer.

She had been a victim of capitalism all her young life. Sleeping under a vegetable cart at twelve years of age, she often did not actually know from where her next meal might come. As she bathed in a nearby stream, she would often wipe tears from her young eyes, wondering forlornly how her parents could bring so many children into a world of want, a world where the Catholic Church was allied with capitalism in her native Philippines, encouraging people to prodigiously reproduce so that there would be a vast array of people desperate for jobs; and thereby, wages would be depressed. Rich people were smart enough to have only two children, although they could afford many more. Not so the poor, because they were all slaves to religion that said be fruitful and multiply. They actually believed one day the first would be last and the last would be first, and that they would walk those streets of gold up in that magical place in the sky.

After three of her sisters died as a result of poverty, she discreetly placed condoms on her parents' bed, hoping they would get the idea they were being foolish bringing so many children into a world of want. She would find them unopened in the trashcan the next day. She kept putting them back on the bed, until one day her mother said, "Lynton, stop the condom routine, we are a

J. Wayne Frye

Catholic family and we must follow the dictates of the church – no birth control."

Shaking her head, Lynton said, "Mom, the church is full of orders for bringing children into the world, but where is the church when those children are starving? Where is the church when the children need health care? Where is the church when the children need an education the parents cannot afford? I doubt if the Pope or any priests ever go hungry, go without healthcare, go without an education, because what we throw in the collection plate takes care of them."

Her mom moved deliberately toward her, and after years of physical abuse, Lynton knew what was coming. A slap across the face stung her like a bevy of bees. Still, despite the pain, she did not cry, did not even whimper, because she was a girl of stern stuff fostered by years of occasional abuse that rather than breaking her actually made her stronger, made her more stubborn, more determined than ever to stand against the tyranny of people like her mom who thought simply because she was a mother she had the right to use and abuse her children, and that no matter how she treated them they were duty bound to respect her, because that was what the Bible said, "Honour thy father and mother."

Once, when her mother told her that, she replied, "What about the parent honouring the child? The child does not ask to be born. That happens as a result of parents getting horny one night – pure and simple." The slap was so hard that time she was knocked across the room into a wall where she hit an exposed nail, and the scar on her right forehead was still there after all these years. It had never healed properly, because her parents could not afford to take her to the hospital. Her loving father had consoled her, working feverishly to stem the flow of blood, as her mom said, "Jesus doesn't like a smart mouth. You got what you deserved."

As Lynton grew toward womanhood, she realized her siblings would starve if she did not figure out a way to feed them, so she took a vegetable cart and hawked her father's meagre crops on the streets. Still, she never missed school, because she was determined that some day, somehow she would claw her way out of the poverty that imprisoned so many in her native Philippines, a poverty compounded by American dominance that insisted on a commitment to capitalism, despite it being a system that guaranteed poverty for the many so the few could enjoy lives of luxurious splendour on the backs of those who were wage-slaves.

She had no memory of the long ago prosperous times, only the stories told her by Filipinos about the once most affluent nation in Asia being turned over to an oligarchy supported by the USA that imprisoned the population to serve the needs of those at the top of the economic ladder. It was not just her native Philippines, but most of the world that was ruled by an oligarchy, which was so firmly entrenched that she saw her only hope was an escape to a nation where there was more economic justice. Singing in a casino lounge in Vancouver, British Columbia, a movie producer friend introduced her to novelist, Wayne Frye, and the spark was lit between them that turned into a raging inferno of passion and adoration, love so consuming that despite the vast age difference between them they were like teenagers falling in love for the first time. They became inseparable.

That love affair is not the subject of this book, and it has been chronicled in many other Lynton adventures, so suffice it to simply say that love affair was why, after six years together, she was finally coming to Canada after spending three years with her husband in Cape Town, South Africa, where she attended a renowned university. She had previously attended Cambridge School of Law on scholarship, but her penchant for the hospitality field led Wayne to encourage her to get a degree in hospitality management.

Finally in Canada, she was nervous, because she had been reading up on the type questions asked by immigration officers when you first arrived. It was common knowledge that it could take up to two hours to get through immigration. As she stood in line, her heart was pumping rapidly while the people were being moved to desk after desk. She knew that her dear Wayne was anxiously waiting downstairs with his friend Bruce. This was the culmination of a dream that she and Wayne had shared for six years, the dream of the two of them being in Canada together.

As she approached the first immigration desk, she said to the officer, "Salut comment allez-vous." ("How are you today" in French.)

He replied, as he looked at her papers and passport, "Ah, parles francais. Tres inhabituel pour un Philippin." ("Ah, you speak French. Very unusual for a Filipino.")

She said in French, "Part of my studies included French. My teacher would be proud."

As he stamped her passport and papers, he said, "And well your teacher should be proud of you. Your French is excellent." With a broad smile, he continued, "Welcome to Canada." That was it!

As was customary for her, she had so charmed a person that what was supposed to be a tedious process was a breeze. Smiling with great joy, she gingerly pushed the cart containing her luggage. She was thrilled that her intense desire to be a resident in the land she had always dreamed about was finally being realized, and waiting downstairs was her husband, who, himself, had sixteen years before left the USA in search of true freedom in a nation that kept the wall between church and state inviolate, offered genuine freedom rather than the highly propagandized variety in America, made healthcare a right rather than privilege and refused to spend foolishly on weapons of war to subdue other countries. This, to her, was like a dream come true. Was she just dreaming? If she was, she did not want to wake up.

Looking down at the lobby far below, she saw Wayne's friend Bruce waiting anxiously. He was as excited about her arrival as Wayne, because the two of them had become grand friends also. He was the person who had stood by Wayne in his darkest hour. He was her friend too, because through the magic of modern technology they talked regularly on Facebook. She was in no way surprised that he had taken the ferry with Wayne from Vancouver Island to the airport in downtown Vancouver to greet her.

She wondered where Wayne was, but figured his intense penchant for sweets might have made him head over to the airport Tim Horton's for some treats, since he figured it would take a couple of hours for her to get through immigration. Little did he know she had worked her usual magic and mesmerized the officer with her sweetness and beauty to speed things up. With Lynton there was a special quality that disarmed the most strident of people, made them like putty in her hands. Wayne and Bruce both knew that so very well.

As she wound her way down the walkway toward the lower lobby, she was breathing heavily with anticipation. She moved to the automatic doors and there was Bruce waiting for her as they swung open. Bruce is that special kind of man with a hulking 150 kilos (over 300 pounds) frame that makes him look intimidating, but he is really just a sweet, lovable teddy bear whose voice is never above a whisper. His quiet, gentle nature belies the gruff looking exterior. He greeted her with a big hug, and then pointed toward Wayne in the far corner, where he was talking to a young beautiful woman.

Lynton said to Bruce, "That's my husband! Leave him alone for a minute, and he will find a beautiful woman to converse with."

Wayne caught Lynton out of the corner of his eyes and encouraged his lady-friend to meet her. As they moved toward Lynton, she smiled her disarming smile and embraced him with great affection.

"I cannot believe you got through immigration so quickly," Wayne said.

"Well, when you are as charming as I am, they can't wait to admit you to Canada, especially if you are a French speaking Filipino. Aren't you going to introduce me to your friend?"

Now, let's make one thing clear. Wayne is an admirer of women, but never has he been one to cheat on a spouse or lover. He is simply, as he told Lynton many times, a man who admires the architecture of a woman, because a woman is not just the roadmap to desire, but the grand and glorious manifestation of the grandeur of a world where a person of the female persuasion is the walking, breathing embodiment of all that gives form function. Oh, and does he love the female form.

Lynton, not afflicted with jealousy, always told Wayne, "Look all you want, but if you touch, then you will be begging for mercy from me!" And she was the girl who could make that promise reality with a fury. Her famous high heels from hell had dispatched many a villain, as had her devastating left hook. Was Wayne scared of the 5:2, fifty kilo (110 pounds) dynamic dynamo? You bet he was!

Wayne said, "This is Sue Fong."

It was obvious to Lynton that she was Chinese-Canadian, so she said hello in Mandarin, much to Sue's surprise. Speaking seven languages fluently and another four semi-fluently, Lynton was a person who had learned them as part of her jobs in hotels over the years.

Wayne said, "Sue is from Ladysmith and just got in from Beijing."

Smiling at Sue, Lynton said, "Leave it to my dear husband to get lucky enough to run into a beautiful woman from his hometown on a visit to the Vancouver airport." Almost giggling now, she continued, "I have noticed his luck is consistent the world over."

Smiling in return, Sue replied, "Well, I consider being told I am beautiful a real compliment from such a stunning woman, and according to Wayne you have brains to match your beauty."

"I've got him fooled about the brains. He is easy to manipulate."

Bruce, knowing Sue also, said to her, "Lynton is right about Wayne's luck. I am not really his friend. Got him fooled! I just know if I hang around with him, eventually I'll meet a beautiful lady."

Laughing together, the four of them headed for the exit and the sky train, and then on to the ferry for the two hour ride to Vancouver Island, a place that was magical to Lynton, despite having only been there for a short while previously over the Christmas holidays from school, and it had been everything Wayne had so vividly described to her as a place of grandeur and beauty, a true Xanadu of magnificence that pulsated with pristine splendour.

Making instant friends with Sue, she and Lynton were walking side by side as they boarded the ferry. The two of them giggled as the two men struggled to be as gentlemanly as possible and were gallantly carrying their heavy suitcases.

Noticing Lynton staring at the stern of the ship, Sue turned to her and said, "What is wrong?"

Always psychically attuned, Lynton gazed at what was more a shadow than a man, a black, menacing-looking shadow at the stern of the ship and said, "Do you see that dark shadow at the stern?"

Looking diligently, Sue replied, "I see it, yes. Oh my, oh my, I see it as I have before and you see it, too. Thank goodness, because I thought I was crazy for years now. But what is it doing here?"

Sue, downcast and shaken with fear, grabbed Lynton's arm, shivering in near delirium. Blinking her eyes as she stared at the stern of the ship, Lynton saw nothing now, but the image, the eerie nature of the image was still in her mind, as if it had been there for either her or Sue, or both of them to see as a warning.

Chapter 1
Titillated Her Inquisitive Mind

Death must be so beautiful,
To lie in the soft brown earth,
With the grasses waving above one's head,
And listen to nothing but silence,
To have no yesterday and no tomorrow,
To forget time, to forget life, to be at peace.
But for some, death does not evil cease,
For there are those dead
Who do not rest in peace.
They are the wanderers
Angry that life has ended.
Be weary of the dark shadows,
Because they feed on fear,
And make things unclear.

The four travellers sat down, without Lynton or Sue mentioning the incident that had occurred while boarding the ship. However, Wayne was an astute observer of people, and knew that something was bothering them. He said, "O.K., what is it with you two? I can see consternation on your faces."

They related to Wayne and Bruce how they both observed a strange, shadowy figure at the stern of the ship as they boarded. Wayne, a chronicler of Lynton's adventures with the supernatural, said, "Oh no, here we go. Not even settled in yet and it has started. Darling, it is bad enough dealing with your precognition, now you have Sue seeing things." He then turned to Bruce, shaking his head. "Get ready for another adventure into the supernatural."

Lynton looked at Sue and said, "I worry my husband way too much, but I must ask you about something you said when we saw that black shadow. You intonated you have seen it before."

"I have, yes. I have seen it twice in Ladysmith. Once at the annual Christmas light up parade just about a five years ago. I was standing on the street watching the parade. As a large decorated truck rolled by, I looked at the crowd across the street and saw that shadowy figure standing behind a First Nations woman I knew. She was a casual acquaintance. He placed his hand on her shoulder, and a week or so later, I found out she had simply disappeared. Her family has tried for many years to find out exactly what happened, but neither they nor the police could find any clues. I informed the police of what I saw, but it led to nothing."

You could see intense interest was obvious as Sue continued with her story. "Then, I was with my First-Nations' friend Luna at the downtown bakery about two years later, and as we sat there at around 5:00 PM, and I am sure that you know it gets dark in the winter here around 4:30, I looked out the window and there looking in was that same black shadowy figure, with a dark hood pulled over its head and all you could make out were fiery red eyes staring intently at my casual acquaintance, Luna. That night, Luna's teenage daughter never came home after an end of school year Christmas party at the high school. I again told the police what I knew, but by then they apparently thought I was bonkers, always seeing this shadowy figure before something bad happened. All those years ago now and no leads in either case."

Lynton said, as she looked at Wayne, who from his facial expression was beginning to show concern about her getting involved again with an adventure that would cause him worry, "Did I say I was getting involved in anyway? I am in Canada to start my new life after three years of intense study. I will be starting a job in a few weeks, and I have no time for adventures into the supernatural. What Sue saw is probably just coincidence, and what we saw tonight was probably, without a doubt, just a lone passenger strolling about the ship."

Lynton and the Ladysmith Phantom

Wayne could see the intense concern on Sue's face. He also knew that Lynton's penchant for sticking her cute little flat Asian nose into things best left alone was just part of her adorable personality. Still, he decided to let the subject drop, took Lynton's hand, squeezed it gently and smiled lovingly at her, as he reflected on her demon hunting over the years that helped make him a successful writer as the chronicler of her adventures. She was more than a source of book royalties to him. He had gone through times of great worry, as she dealt not just with the supernatural, but with real living evil in the hearts of men and women who knew no boundaries in their pursuit of ill-gotten gains in a capitalist world that taught people that money bought happiness, and that the accumulation of wealth was a measure of a person's worth. This was the evil of the vilest economic system ever devised, a system that relegated billions to poverty while the few lived in luxurious grandeur. She shared his disdain for the material things of life, his sincere questioning of the economic order that relegated far too many to the outside looking in, and also his penchant to question the hypocrisy of the church. Still, the world also was a place where evil lurked about with great rapidity, the simple evil of those who enjoyed seeing people tremble in fear. Apparently, this shadowy figure was one of those that enjoyed instilling fear.

After leaving Vancouver, long before you come to the city of Nanaimo on Vancouver Island

J. Wayne Frye

the ferry streams through a sea that enters a region of singular loneliness and desolation, where its waters spread away on all sides, and the grandeur of the beautiful island begins to come into view. It assaults the senses as you approach it from the open sea. The magnificence of the fantastic colouring of the beaches in the distance massaged Lynton's eyes with the soft serenity of a magical land a mere 25 kilometres from a bustling metropolis; a land she had visualized for years, but her imagination had been lacking, because before her lay paradise in a land she already loved. Above the tide-line, the grey rocks were splashed with intense yellow that soothed the soul. All around them were the vivid orange-browns and sienna of seaweeds, and upon the rocks stretched out in repose were the brownish sea lions, as if they were mighty kings and queens on thrones. The water through which they gracefully glided was crystal clear, so clear she, looking out the window, could see her reflection. The waves were gentle but rolling with salty white crystal spray at the crests. She felt as if she were not coming to a new place, but to an old home that had been in her mind all her life. The grandeur of this place was overwhelming as Wayne wrapped his left arm around her, pulling her to him. It was like being wrapped in a warm blanket on a cold night. She was adored, and she revelled in the adoration of a man she, likewise, adored.

In the high-tide of life, Lynton saw this island as the finest place on earth, a place that would welcome her into the bosom of comfort. She felt at home, felt like this was the culmination of a life-long dream that freed her from the backwardness of the Philippines, which had become, because of American economic interference, a land every bit as trapped by an oligarchy as the USA. Her three years in South Africa were a respite, where she dutifully prepared for what was happening at this very moment. It was a time when she and Wayne learned to cohabitate in harmony with one another in preparation for their life in Canada. Yet, she could not get her mind off that dark shadowy figure. Try as hard as she could, the image kept popping into her mind, but she vowed not to say anything to Wayne about her consternation.

Arriving at Duke Point Ferry Terminal at dusk, which was 20 minutes from Ladysmith, the four of them walked to the parking lot where they said goodbye to Sue as darkness sat eerily in. It was obvious that Sue had her mind on that solitary lone dark figure, as she bid them all adieu.

Lynton's new home

J. Wayne Frye

Lynton and the Ladysmith Phantom

Racing along at one hundred kilometres an hour in Bruce's rumbling truck, within a few minutes they were in Ladysmith with Bruce taking the downtown route so Lynton could enjoy the quaint beauty of the place she now called home. Although downtown, there was a sense of remoteness from the world of humankind, an utter isolation in a singular world of arbutus, cedars, gentle wind and about 500 metres from downtown the calm waters of the bay. All this instantly laid its spell upon Lynton, so that she smiled at Wayne as she nestled up to him and sighed. She felt she was in a little kingdom of wonder and magic, a kingdom that was welcoming her to quiet serenity, with everywhere unwritten solicitations of hope for a bright tomorrow in the warm, caring arms of the man she loved.

Though fairly early in the evening, the darkness was like a sudden creeping torrent with the steady, ceaseless buffetings of a moderately tempestuous wind that was stirring about with a weary whine. The wind was buffeting against Bruce's truck, but as they cruised through the brightly lit downtown the wind ceased, almost as if someone had magically snapped their fingers and commanded it to do so.

Leaving Main Street behind, Bruce cruised up the inclining road until he arrived at the intersection and turned right, heading up the long, winding hill to Wayne's house halfway down the side of a pristine mountain, where the two climbed out of the truck and said goodbye to Bruce.

Lynton and Wayne stood there at the top of the driveway, looking out at the grandeur all about them. In the far distance to their left, the Whistler Ski Resort on the mainland had the bright lights on getting ready for night-time skiing that started in December as the slopes were a popular allure for those who loved the fine, soft, powdery snow for which the resort was so famous. Then, the two of them turned and walked back toward the house hand-in-hand, with the full moon shining down brightly on their home as if anointing it with the moonlight of hope.

Lynton's new home – Bay View Chateau

Perhaps some people are natural magnets for adventure. Lynton, apparently, is one of those who simply seem to always fall into situations that others willingly avoid. Maybe it is her naturally curious nature that makes her so inquisitive about things that others would simply walk away from with a shrug of the shoulders. Her recent adventure chronicled in the book, *Lynton and the Haunting of the HMS Wind Dancer,* had been the most harrowing of her entire 34 years, and she had vowed it would be her last. Yet, as she cuddled up to Wayne, she could not get that lone dark shadowy figure on the deck of the ferry out of her mind. And what of the other two times Sue had seen that ominous-looking manifestation?

She drifted off to sleep, comfortable in the arms of the man who had changed her life; the same man who had pleaded with her to move on and forget him because of their age difference. She told him that love has no age barriers, and that if it did not bother her it should not bother him. Getting him to the altar took all her wily ingenuity, but she was a woman who never let any barrier stand in her way, as when she made up her mind about something that was it. There simply was no stopping her from reaching any objective.

So many times things happened to Lynton that had never happened to anyone else. Thus was the nature of the woman affectionately called the dynamic dynamo by so many. It should be firmly stated that she is more than just a woman; she is a phenomena of nature, a hurricane force of kindness and sympathy for the downtrodden and the trauma afflicted of a world where compassion is in short supply, a world where the many are perpetual slaves to the few who exact complete control over the lesser among us, a world that has its priorities askew and effectively utilizes propaganda to keep the populace in ignorance, so they will never challenge the authority of the religious oligarchy, the rich and well-connected.

Lynton had battled all her life against bowing before the banality of people manipulated by religion and/or government propaganda that makes it understandable how mass ignorance has people lining up for their own balls and chains. For example, she marvelled at how all types of abominations are tolerated by most Americans when the flag is waved or the name of Jesus is invoked. How could lovers of Jesus tolerate allowing the American government to take suckling babies from mothers' arms and lock the two of them in separate cages simply because they illegally crossed a border in hopes of gaining a bit of that freedom Americans so brazenly brag about? And what of the millions of homeless on the streets, the lack of medical care, the gross income inequality, the attack on freedom of the press that brands anything not in support of the promotion of ignorance for the masses as fake news or the obscene arrogance that brands Americans as some how exceptional? She had been but a child when she observed the Philippines go from the lion of Asia to a dutiful pussy cat domesticated by corporate America, watching her homeland descend into abject poverty for the many while the few were allowed

J. Wayne Frye

to live in splendorous luxury. This was a woman who simply refused to accept the fate so many of her brethren had. She was not a slave to capitalism, nor was she a slave to the moneyed oligarchy that ruled the Philippines and most of the world. She refused to bow before authority.

I say that because perhaps the things that will be revealed here could only have happened to a person with Lynton's depth of character. As I look back over her life as mentioned previously, when a child she suffered so much abject poverty as a result of parents who were too religious to practice birth control that she was forced to leave home at 12, so they would have one less mouth to feed. She understood even at that age that more people meant more slaves to the corporate machinery that looked upon people as commodities rather than human beings. She had a few well-intentioned people take her under their wings, and she eventually joined the managerial class and managed to go to the Cambridge School of Law. Then, giving up a managerial position at a spa chain, she went to South Africa, where she attended the International Hotel School. Now, she had joined her husband in Canada and already had a managerial job at an exclusive private boarding school, and was about to start an on-line second Master's degree from Harvard University. This was an exceptional woman, about to get herself in a parcel of trouble.

Now that we have familiarized ourselves with Lynton, let's get familiar with Sue Fong. She was of Chinese ancestry on her father's side, but she had been born in Canada into very wealthy circumstances. She, like Lynton, was somewhat of an anomaly. She had been told that her parents died in an automobile accident when she was a baby, but she found out the truth years later, which will be related eventually. A bevy of relatives took care of her. Unfortunately, most were doing it, not out of love, but out of a desire to ingratiate themselves to a girl who one day would come into all the vast wealth left by her parents.

She was a precocious and intelligent child who very early began to wonder if she were not different from other children. That was, of course, largely because the near castle high atop a mountain overlooking Ladysmith was imposing, and the exclusive private school she attended was the very one where Lynton was about to take a position. Her shyness and fear of the dark shadows she often saw about the elaborate estate were ever present in her mind, and she usually begged one of the many servants to sleep on the sofa in her bedroom, as she also sensed those dark shadows flittering about late at night there.

A certain clannish etiquette made it seem necessary that many of her relations from Vancouver should pay her a visit sometimes, because she, despite her age, was very important based upon her future wealth possibilities. The huge, frowning estate standing upon its rock foundation on the side of a mountain was hers, but everything was managed by lawyers. She was a great heiress, and despite her young age she was, so to speak, the head of the extended family. As a youth she was a budding beauty, although somewhat undersized, but had no attraction whatsoever for anyone but Dina Layette, a distant older cousin, who took care of her, and Angus Agnore, who looked after the elaborate library at the estate, and who was assumed to be a distant relative also.

They were both like her in the fact that they were not given to speech; but sometimes they talked to one another, and she knew they were fond of her, as she was fond of them. They were really all she had, as at school she felt sorely out-of-place and even pleaded to go to public school in Ladysmith, but was told by the lawyers, who managed the estate, that it was inappropriate for someone of her station in life to attend public school. Hey, after all, the moneyed class could not mingle with the poor peons, the great unwashed masses that were put on earth to serve the needs of the aristocracy. And even in a more equalitarian society like Canada, there were still definite class distinctions; although they were not nearly as pronounced as in the United States. The nice thing about Sue was that she did not ascribe to any class distinctions whatsoever, despite her executors unequivocal determination to force them upon her. Yet, she had to yield to the executors on most decisions due to the stipulation in her parents' will that she would not be allowed full control of the estate until her twenty-fifth birthday.

When she was a little girl and then a young adult, she lived in forced opulence, but never embraced it with anything but the realization she had no choice. For her, life was simply not that pleasurable, because she was so restrained by the executors of the estate that she actually had very little freedom and few friends.

All this time her growing beauty made her a woman of interest for many young men, but she actually had little to do with any of them, because her lawyers were always cautioning her that most men were simply interested because of her vast wealth.

Her life was a peculiar one, but the strangest part of it was that while she was at the head of so many people she did not really have an affinity for any of them, nor did she take much counsel from anyone except the aforementioned forced-by-the-will advice of her attorneys. At 24, she had only ten more months until she could fire them, and take over the management of the estate herself. It was a time she was looking forward to, not so she could get her hands on all that wealth, but because she wanted to feel in control of her own destiny free of the imposed will of those she saw as a restraint on her freedom.

One of her earliest memories was once hearing through a closed door a servant say to another servant, "Both her father and mother were dead when she was born." She did not even know that was a remarkable thing to say until she was many years older and another servant, in confidence, told her what had been meant and how her parents had really died. It seems that her father and mother had both been very young and both born into great wealth. They apparently came to Ladysmith, because family lived across the bay in Vancouver and encouraged them to do so. They lived in a hundred year old very dark and foreboding mansion on the hillside away from the town. Most times they were quite alone and spent their days fishing or riding or wandering about the vast mountain estate together, or reading by the fire in the library the ancient books their librarian, Angus Agnore, found for them. The library was a marvellous place, and Agnore knew every volume in it. His employers used to sit and read like children the vast collection of fairy stories, and then they would persuade Agnore to tell them the ancient tales he knew of the days when Ladysmith was nothing but wild wilderness with bears, elk, cougars and other beasts roaming about freely, as he had a great grandfather who was a trapper and had lived in the wilds, but as civilization encroached he moved further up the mountain and beyond the reach of the growing town as he saw freedom diminishing when men became dependent on others for their sustenance. His own father had turned his back on the wild life and migrated to Vancouver, where Angus went to the University of British Columbia and studied to be a librarian. After getting his Ph.D., he, remembering his roots, longed to be free of the growing jungle of concrete and steel in Vancouver and returned to

Ladysmith, when he received word that a wealthy family was looking for a librarian to curate their personal estate library.

Sue did not know how it was that she seemed to see her young father and mother so clearly and to know how radiant and wildly in love they were. Surely the servants who had known them had some words to tell her. Learning what really happened was shocking, but she was glad to understand, in a way, what happened to her mother one day in late November when her father was brought home dead, followed by the guests who had gone out shooting with him. His foot had caught in a gopher hole, and his shotgun had fallen to the ground and discharged just as he slumped from the pain, shooting him in the face, almost obliterating it from the chin up. He died right there on the spot. One moment he had been the wealthy, handsome owner of a vast estate and the next a corpse on the sofa in the foyer with a sheet covering what was left of his face, so Sue's mom would not have to endure the agony of seeing her husband's shattered remains.

Sue's mom never asked to see his body, because she was on the bedroom balcony which juts over the rock the house is built on, and which looks out over the lower vestiges of the estate. She saw from there the returning party of hunters winding their way slowly through the open area above the cedar trees, following a burden carried on a stretcher of coats and two boughs from a pine tree. Some of her women guests were with her, and one of them said afterward that when Sue's mother first caught sight of the moving figures she slowly crept to the edge of the balcony on the left side of the house with a crouching movement almost like a cougar preparing to spring. But she only watched, making neither sound nor movement until the cortege was near enough for her to see that her husband was not visible, which only could mean he was the lifeless figure on the stretcher. Then she said quite slowly and with a tone of acceptance, "it has killed him," and fell upon the floor like a dropped stone.

It was because of this that the servant had said that Sue's mother was dead when she was born. It must have seemed almost as if she were not a living thing. She did not open her eyes or make a sound; she laid white and cold waiting for the birth. The celebrated physicians who came from Victoria in the south of the island talked of catalepsy and afterward wrote scientific articles which tried to explain her condition. She did know when Sue was born, but was too weak to even look upon her. She gave birth to a little girl who would never know love and affection from her mother or father.

Much later, after Sue found out the truth, Dina Layette told her that she had knelt by her mother's bed after the birth to hold her hand and watched her with eyes that were so near her every moment that she saw a thing the others there did not know her well enough, or love her well enough, to see. The first few minutes she was like a dead thing that had never lived. But when the hand of the clock passed the last second, and the new hour began, Dina bent closer to her because she saw a change stealing over her. It was scary. Dina turned and looked behind her, as it appeared that was where Sue's mother's eyes were focused. She saw in the dark corner of the room a kind of misty shadow like outline. She assumed that if she had spoken of what she thought she saw the others there would have said she was light-headed with grief and have sent her away. Until this very moment with Sue, she had never told man or woman what she saw. She then leaned in close to little Sue and said, "I can tell you that the change I saw was as if she was beginning to be engrossed with fear, not of death but of that infernal thing in the corner. But then she lay content, and slowly began to slip away, as whatever it was in that room, seemed to still be there. I have postulated that perhaps it, that thing in the corner, was the soul of your father, waiting for your birth, and then waiting for your dear mother to finally slip away and join him, because once I knew she was dead I turned and the thing was gone."

Sue, after that revelation from Dina, began to stand on the very balcony of the bedroom where her mother had seen her father's body being brought from below. That soon became a regular place for her to stand, look out upon the vast estate and contemplate. She began to think the forest below was her secret companion and friend, that it was not only an estate to her, but something else.

Lynton and the Ladysmith Phantom

It was like a thing alive, a huge giant lying spread out in the sun warming itself below or covering itself with thick, white mist in the mornings which sometimes writhed and twisted into a wraith. First she noticed and liked it some days, perhaps, when it was purple and yellow with heather and broom, and the honey scents drew bees and butterflies and birds. But soon she saw and was drawn by another thing more sinister.

She was maybe 16 that afternoon when she sat on the lone balcony chair and watched the low, soft whiteness creeping out and hovering over the broom bushes as if the forest itself had breathed it up from the rich loam of the earth? It was such a low little mist at first; and it crept and crept until its creeping grew into something heavier and whiter, and it began to hide the heather and the broom and then the low young fir trees. It mounted and mounted, and sometimes a breath of wind twisted it into weird shapes, almost like human creatures cavorting about. It opened and closed again, and then it dragged and crept and grew thicker. And as she inquisitively leaned forward, it mounted still higher and got hold of the forest and hid it, hanging heavy and white as if waiting, waiting and waiting. Then it came into her mind that it had done what the forest had told it to do; had hidden things which wanted to be hidden, and then it waited, waited, waited. Oh, how it waited, and when that white morning mist eventually disappeared still Sue would never venture below.

Lynton and the Ladysmith Phantom

A few days later Sue invited Lynton over for tea and related to her all of the above, detailing for her the unknown fear to never wander about the forest below to the area where her father was killed.

Lynton wanted to avoid any entanglements with the supernatural, because she had promised Wayne that her days as a demon hunter were over, but then again this was not about just a demon. It was about a new friend in need, a person who needed understanding, sympathy and compassion.

As Lynton looked out upon the forest below, she had a vague feeling that there was some strange life there that one could not exactly see, but she was conscious of something being there, because she had a sixth sense. She felt that there was definitely something amiss, something that titillated her inquisitive mind.

Chapter 2
The Abyss

You shiver in the darkness
With the black shadows of doubt.
The fear curdles the blood
And the cold can be felt all about.

Death is not the end for some,
Because they refuse to give up life.
To them darkness is a delight,
Where they are able to spread strife.

Lynton asked Sue if she thought the dark shadowy figure she had seen three times now was that same one seen by her mother and Dina so many years ago. She replied, "I am not sure. It well could be I suppose. There is something strange about the way Dina and Angus are always keeping a close eye on me. I do know that there is something Dina and Angus may not have shared out of fear it might cause me consternation."

Looking quizzically at Sue, Lynton said, "Are Dina and Angus fond of each other in their silent way?"

"They are I believe," replied Sue

"Explain," said Lynton.

"Well," offered Sue, "I was kept in the open air a great deal. Angus would walk by my side, always plodding along with me. Generally, Dina would accompany us. Never, of course, would they walk with me down toward the area where my father was killed and borne by the other hunters to the house. Perhaps that was because they sensed it was too painful, too traumatic for me. We always worked our way up the side of the mountain, not down. Often we set out early in the morning, and some simple food was carried so that we need not return to the house until we chose. We would walk until I found a place I liked; then Dina and Angus would sit down among the trees, and I would wander about and play in my own way."

At this point, Sue took a deep breath, and Lynton said, "Is this leading to the answer to my question?"

Smiling, Sue replied, "Be patient. Anyway, I think I must have played as almost any lonely little girl might have played. I used to find a corner among the bushes and pretend it was my house, and that I had little friends who came to play with me. I only remember one thing which was not like the ordinary playing of children. It was a habit I had of sitting quite still a long time and listening. That was what I called it – listening. I was listening to hear if the life in the forest made any sound I could understand. I felt as if it might, if I were very still and listened long enough. While waiting for the sounds one day, I looked to my right and through a maybe 300 metre tunnel-like opening amongst a thick grove of trees I could see Dina and Angus far in the distance. They were passionately embracing, kissing again and again. That was over 15 years ago, and I never saw it happen again. I am not saying it has not happened; only I have not seen it since. Still, there is an intensity between them. They do not touch, do not make any conversation about endearment to one another, but I sense there is something there. Why they do not just come out with it I do not know, unless it is fear that my executors might fire them."

"What about other incidents, ones that maybe did not involve any indication of intimacy?"

"Well, Angus and Dina and I were not afraid of rain and mist and change of weather. If they had been we could have had little outdoor life. We always carried extra wraps enough to keep us warm and dry if bad weather presented itself. So one day we did not turn back when we found ourselves in the midst of a sudden thick mist. We sat down in a sheltered place under a canopy of trees and waited, knowing it would lift in time, because the sun had been shining when we set out, and, no doubt would do so again. Of that we were all three sure."

"Angus and Dina were content to sit and guard me while I amused myself. They knew I would keep near them and run into no danger. I was not an adventurous child. I was, in fact, in a more than usually quiet mood that morning. The quiet had come upon me when the mist had begun to creep about and enclose us. I liked it. I liked the sense of being shut in by the soft whiteness I had so often watched from the balcony. I told Angus that maybe some other people were out in the forest, as I could hear the soft sound of feet on the ground, but he assured me there was no noise at all."

"I played very little that day. The quiet and the mist held me still. Soon I sat down and began to intently listen. After a while I knew that Dina and Angus were watching me, but it did not disturb me in the least. They often watched me when they thought I did not know they were doing so."

Sue took a long deep breath and continued. "I had sat listening for nearly half an hour when I heard the first muffled, slow trampling of debris on the forest floor. I knew what it was even before it drew near enough for me to be conscious of the other sounds, the strides of a large person walking. The sounds were faint and distant at first but soon they were really quite near. They did sound eerie, but I was not afraid. Dina and Angus did not

J. Wayne Frye

appear to hear them. I assumed that I only heard them, because I had been so intensely listening."

"Out of the mist strode a tall, dark figure wearing long garments such as I had never seen before, garments from days of old, very old. It was very similar to the garment on that dark figure I have seen over the years. Maybe it was that dark figure. Although I could not make it out, I immediately assumed it was something savage and uncouth. There was also a smell, the smell of blood all about. I did not know or even ask myself why the situation did not frighten me, but it did not. I stood there in awe of this large thing moving my way. I turned and looked back at Angus and Dina. They were apparently totally unaware of what was unfolding before me. Suddenly I seemed to know that I was probably facing something evil, but I was so mesmerized that I could not scream, could not cry out for help from the two people about 100 metres behind me. Still, apparently Angus and Dina did not see or hear anything, as they sat quietly in contemplation."

Again, Sue sighed long and very deeply, as she continued. "The thing in the dark garment was a lean figure with an incredibly determined stride that seemed to say within that robe beat the heart of a giant among people, a thing that demanded fear from all before it. That menacing-looking, black, ominous vision kept striding with determination my way, and then somewhat afraid, I was unable to move, despite wanting to run to Angus and Dina."

"At that point the strangest thing occurred, as a small girl a few years older than I appeared in a mist to the left of the rather ominous seeming creature. She stood there silently, raising her right hand indicating the thing should halt its forward motion. She was wearing a brown dress with embroiders on it. There was a dark-red stain on the left of the dress. She had brown hair and soft soulful eyes. I saw her and instantly liked her for some unknown reason. Still, Angus and Dina said nothing, did nothing, indicating they saw nothing of the two figures. The dark shadowy figure had been staid by one motion from the little girl. It turned and began to stride away, but it strode with a great reluctance, as if it had not wanted to leave me, not wanted to stop trying to instil me with fear. I sensed it was disappointed that the little girl had come along. Still, Angus and Dina said and did nothing."

The sigh from Sue was longer and more pronounced this time. "Of course, I know how strange this seems, but that cannot be helped and does not really matter. It was in that way the thing happened and it did not even seem that strange to me afterwards. What was most strange was that my two companions heard and saw nothing. Anything might happen in that forest, Lynton. It is a strange place."

"And what of the girl?"

"I knew she had come to play with me, and we went together to an area among the bushes of broom and played happily with Angus and Dina watching, but apparently they only saw me, not the other girl. But I saw the girl stand and look wonderingly at the dark-red stain on her dress. The stain was almost directly over her heart. It was as if she was asking herself how it came there and could not understand. Then she picked a small fern from a bunch of thick-growing plants, placing them in her waistband in such a way that it hid the ugliness of the thick blood stains. I did not really know how long she stayed. I only knew that we were apparently happy but silent. Though her way of playing was in some ways different from mine, I enjoyed being with her. Presently the mist lifted and the sun shone, and we were deep in a wonderful game of hiding. She ran behind a big broom bush and did not come back. Then, a strange noise was heard, a kind of moaning. When I ran to look for her she was nowhere. I could not find her, and I went, with a perplexed countenance, back to Dina and Angus."

"Where did she go I asked Dina and Angus, turning my head from side to side? They were looking at me strangely, and both of them were pale. They replied, 'She who?' as if surprised."

"The little girl the dark figure must have brought to play with me I answered, as I looked about inquisitively."

"The two of them said, 'We saw nothing. We heard nothing,' which shocked me."

"I was on the verge of uncontrollable anger, but let it drop. Although they claimed not to see or hear anything that day, I do believe they knew something they did not share. It was something they feared to tell me."

"Later, I overheard the two of them as we were walking back home, whispering about Dark Malcolm and little Elizabeth."

"Frustrated, I turned and asked Dina where did the little girl go? Then, Dina swept me in her warm, shaking arms and hugged me close to her breast, as she explained that the girl was one of the fair ones, and that I had seen a ghost that had been thought to have left the forest long ago."

"If we three had been different; if we had ever had the habit of talking and asking questions we might surely have asked one another questions as we walked back. But they asked me nothing, and I said very little except that I spoke again of the wild-looking, scary dark figure in the mist and of the little girl's mostly dark mood. The two of them looked at one another perplexed, but said nothing to me or to each other."

"When we got home, Angus, as I was going up the stairs, asked if there had been words spoken between me and the girl."

"I hesitated, and then I shook my head as I realized that we had said no words at all. But I had known what she wanted me to understand, and she had known what I might have said to her if I had spoken, so no words were needed."

"After my bath, Dina sat by my bed until I fell asleep. She was obliged to sit rather a long time, because I was so happy with my memories of who I assume was Elizabeth and the certainty that she would come again. And she did. She came several times. I knew that she would come and play with me, though I never saw the dark figure again, but now I realize it was the same figure I have seen thrice now. At least I believe it to be after some reflection."

Lynton asked, "And when Elizabeth came back, you did not ask her from where she came?"

"Children who play together are not very curious about one another, and I simply accepted her with delight. Somehow I knew that she lived in a place not far away in the forest. She could come and go, it seemed, without trouble, but I did notice that when she disappeared a large bat would appear menacingly in the skies overhead, scanning the area as if in search of prey. The bat scared me."

Lynton, ever perceptive, said, "But she stopped coming didn't she, stopped abruptly.

"She did, yes. I missed her at first, but it was not with a great sense of grief or final loss. She had only gone somewhere, but one day would return I thought. She never did."

"What of your relatives at this time of your life?" asked Lynton?

"Of course my relatives did not really like me. How could they? They were busy in their big world and did not know what to do with a little girl who ought to have been important and was not. I am sure that in secret they were relieved whenever they were free of me. They came because they assumed one day I might lavish them with money if they were nice to me. Stupid people, I will give them nothing."

"After that, the life I lived went on quietly. I studied after school with Angus, and made the book-walled library my own room. I learned more with him among the books than I did in school. I walked in the upper forest, but never wandered to the area where my father had been killed in the mist. I walked the long way around to avoid that area and gradually came to know the people who lived in the cottages below the hill, eventually meeting your husband a few years ago. I think he liked me from the beginning. Of course, why shouldn't he, as I could recite many lines from his books, which surprised him. Still, Angus and Dina were my nearest and dearest friends."

"Angus contacted the mainland book-shops for the best modern books, and I began to read them. I felt at first as if they plunged me into a world I did not understand, and many of them I could not endure. But I persevered, and studied them as I had studied the old ones, and in time I began to feel as if perhaps they were true. My chief weariness with them came from the way they had of referring to the things I was so intimate with as though they were only the unauthenticated history of a life so long passed by that it could no longer matter to anyone. So often, the greatest hours of great lives were treated as possible legends. I knew why men had died or were killed or had borne black horror. I knew because I had read old books and manuscripts and had heard the stories which had come down through centuries by word of mouth, passed on and on."

"But there was one man who did not write as if he believed the world had begun and would end with him. That was your husband. The first time I read a book he had written I caught my breath with great reflective thought, again and again. I knew I had found a friend just down the mountainside. He was a somewhat famous writer, and people around here honoured him; while I, hidden away in my home on a rock, was so far from being interesting or clever that even in my grandest evening dress and tiara of jewels I was as insignificant as a mouse. In fact, I always felt rather silly when I was obliged to wear my diamonds on special occasions as a result of my lawyers demanding it, as they said I needed to show my station in life."

Your husband, in particular, titillated my imagination, as he wrote marvellous stories which always seemed real though they were called fiction. Wheresoever his story was placed, howsoever remote and unknown the scene, it was a real place and the people who lived in it were real, as if he had some magic power to call up human things to breathe and live and set one's heart racing with excitement. I read everything he wrote. I read every word of his again and again. I always kept some book of his near enough to be able to touch it with my hand; and often I sat by the fire in the library holding one open on my lap for an hour or more, only because it meant a warm, close companionship. It seemed at those times as if he sat near me in the dim glow, and we understood each other's thoughts without using words, as Elizabeth and I had understood. Then there were his books featuring you and your demon-fighting skills. Soon, even without having formally met you, I felt that we were kindred spirits. I lived somewhat vicariously through your adventures, but never mentioned it to Wayne. I just praised your skills."

Smiling, Lynton interrupted. "Well, remember that Wayne embellishes to make my adventures seem more exciting than they were."

"He genuinely adores you, but I am sure you know that."

Almost laughing, Lynton relied. "Of course I know. I have to be very careful not to become a spoiled brat, because his love is so intense; however, putting that aside, I need to ask you a pertinent question in regards to, not just the appearance of Elizabeth and the dark figure, but in regards to your relatives and your executors. Are any of them aware of the appearances?

"Absolutely not."

"And neither have you, Angus or Dina ever mentioned them to anybody?"

"Me, definitely no, and although I cannot be 100% sure, I do not believe they have done so either."

"Now," said Lynton, "do not get upset, but sometimes the most minor detail can lead to explanations for a variety of things. What about your love life. Have you had many romantic interests over the years?"

Smiling and in an almost forlorn voice, Sue replied with a sigh, "Very, very boring I am afraid. Everything about my love life is G rated, unfortunately."

"Come on now, girl. There has never been even an inkling of interest on your part? Are you so scared of people only being interested in you because of money that you have never had even a brief romantic fling?"

"Well, I did have an intense interest one time in another writer, a man on the mainland who writes non-fiction. I had seen his picture on the cover of one of his books. He was maybe forty at the time, but so very distinguished looking, a real grey fox he was. I never dreamed of meeting him, but since I was a teenager I had a crush on him. I had felt this way for several years, and every year he had grown more famous, when it happened that one year when I was 22 my executors required me to go to Vancouver to see some other lawyers and sign some important documents connected with the management of the estate. In doing so, while I was in the office waiting to see the attorneys in walks this author, Matthew Drury. It just so happens one of the lawyers in the firm represented him. He sat across from me, and seemed to be genuinely taken with me, and his interest was not predicated on my wealth, because he did not know who I was. Anyway, he obviously had plenty of money himself as a renowned writer and professor of history at the University of British Columbia. When I told him my name, it seemed to have no affect on him whatsoever. He asked if I was going to be in town awhile, and I replied yes, because my executors had arranged for me to attend several soirées in order to mingle among the wealthy and well-connected. That led to him asking me if I was staying at a hotel. When I told him I was, he suggested I stay at his place, as there were many servants and there would me no improprieties.

Lynton said, "Very interesting that he would just happen to be at the attorneys' office when you were."

"Yes, it might seem that way, but now here comes the kicker. Ready? He was an honourable man, and he had a wife!"

"Bummer," interjected Lynton.

"It was indeed, but thus is my love life I am afraid. However, I did enjoy their company, and my executors were actually enthusiastic about it as they were prominent socially, so I would often be invited to their home where other prominent people would be. I did not wish to do them an injustice, so I paid them visits and tried to behave as they wished, much as I disliked dressing in fine clothing and wearing diamonds. It was an odd thing that at this time I found I did not dread the visits to Vancouver as much as I usually did. For some unknown reason I became conscious that I was not really reluctant to go. Usually, the thought of having to go made me restless and low-spirited.

J. Wayne Frye

Lynton and the Ladysmith Phantom

Vancouver always seemed so confused and crowded, and made me feel as if I were being pushed and jostled by a mob always making a tiresome, loathsome noise. It was a curious feeling. I could not help noticing and wondering about it. Then, one time, Dina made the journey with me, and one incident made it momentous. It was sad though as it involved a poor woman who was in mourning. We had been alone in our part of the ferry on the return from Vancouver, when a man in a cloak took a seat across from us, despite there being many empty seats about. To our right, across the large aisle, suddenly appeared an obviously poor woman and her child. The man, who had sat across from us, looked their way with penetrating eyes. His eyes were fiery and deep. He wore a hood, and I could see little but his eyes. The face was obscured. The poor woman was terribly distraught and was crying. It actually made one's heart stand still to see the wild grief of her, and her unconsciousness of the world about her. The world did not matter. There was no world for her now. I think there was nothing left anywhere for her, because based upon the black clothing the two were wearing they had just been to a funeral. It was my guess that it was her child's funeral. I felt as if she had been lying sobbing and writhing and beating with her poor hands the new turf on a fresh grave just awhile before, and I somehow knew that it had been a child's grave. It was because I thought this that I wished she had not seemed so unconscious of and indifferent to the child who was with her and clung to her black dress as if it could not bear to let her go. This one was alive at least, even if she had lost the other one. And its little face was so wistful! It did not seem fair to forget and ignore it, as if it were not there. I felt as if she might have left it behind if it had not clung to her skirt so vehemently. When she sank into her seat she did not even lift the poor little thing into the place beside her, but left it to scramble up as best it could. She buried her swollen face in her handkerchief and sobbed in a smothered way as if she neither saw, heard, nor felt any living thing near her."

"I was on the verge of tears myself at the sad scene. How I wished she would remember the poor child and let it comfort her! It really was trying to do so in its innocent way. It pressed close to her side. It looked up imploringly, and it kissed her arm and her black veil over and over again and tried to attract her attention. It was a little, lily-fair creature not more than five or six years old and perhaps too young to express what it wanted to say. It could only cling to her and kiss her black dress, and seem to beg her to remember that it, at least, was a living thing. But the woman was too absorbed in her anguish to know that this child was even in the world. She neither looked at nor touched it, and at last it sat with its cheek against her sleeve, softly stroking her arm, and now and then kissing it longingly. I was obliged to turn my face away and look out of the window, because I knew the man across from me saw the tears well up into my eyes. As the two of us turned away from the sad scene and looked out the window at the undulating waves, it seemed an hour passed, but, no doubt, it was but a few minutes. And you know what? That child, that little girl that was with the sobbing woman made my heart ache."

"The two of us turned our gaze back towards the sad woman and child at the exact same time. Oh, how frightfully sad the two were. I absolutely seethed with misery for their predicament. Then the man got up, looked at me with those fiery eyes, seemingly boring a hole in me with his stare. He walked away, and as he did I looked over where the woman had been and there was nobody there."

"I said to Dina? 'Wasn't that woman and child so very sad?' To my astonishment, she quizzically replied, 'What woman and child?' I was dumbfounded."

"Dina, who is best described as a very observant woman, a woman so attuned to her surroundings that she rarely misses anything, looked incredibly bewildered by my question. Now, it cannot be said of me that I am a very emotional person in most situations, but I was perturbed that she could have sat there all that time and have not seen the woman and little girl, not observed the intense sorrow that was gripping them both, not have been deeply touched with compassion for two people obviously in intense emotional pain. I was perplexed and ready to scream at the top of my lungs. There is something in us all Lynton that often puts us on a precipice looking over a deep, dark abyss, and we can teeter forward into the abyss, or we can lean back and escape the darkness, the despair, the evil that awaits us in that pit. But, at times, we want to see what waits for us there; what is calling us into that putrid darkness. You know that feeling, because you have gone into the jaws of hell to fight against the demons of darkness. You have dived over the precipice into that dark pit, without fear. At that very moment I was ready to completely let go of my sanity, let go so that I could see into the darkness, dive into that pit and meet whatever fate awaited me, especially when I decided to turn to her and finally asked one more question that would at least let me know I was not on the edge of insanity. I said to her very calmly that those people were no figment of my imagination. I had seen them, and the man sitting across from us had seen them. It was then that I genuinely questioned my sanity, because she interjected words that haunt me to this very day. She said 'what man?' That was it; I had actually dived into the abyss."

J. Wayne Frye

Chapter 3
In My Dream

What is the knocking?
What is the knocking
At the door in the night?
Is it somebody or some thing
That wants to instil fright?

Be ever vigilant of all seen,
But also as vigilant of the unseen,
As knocking sounds the alarm,
Bringing shivers for something
That desires to cause harm!

Lynton left Sue with a promise to find out all she could about the strange manifestations that were plaguing her, as unlike the others, Lynton had apparently seen one of the apparitions on the ferry deck. She knew Wayne would be upset, but Sue was his friend, too, so how could he deny Lynton the opportunity to lend her a hand?

Wayne accepted her determination to find out about the apparent apparitions with a shrug of the shoulders, a sigh and the oft repeated, "Here we go again."

Lynton and Wayne were invited by Sue to a party in Vancouver a relative was giving. However, Wayne was out of town for two weeks on a book tour, so Lynton went alone.

It was there in Vancouver that she met some of Sue's relatives, most of whom she found snobbish and exceedingly arrogant, seeming to dismiss her as "poor Filipino trash" who did not have the proper social status to mingle with the rich and well-connected. Having so often experienced prejudice among the rich and privileged, she never let it bother her, but rather, like her husband, looked at most of those at the top of the economic ladder as leeches that used and abused the working class in order to accumulate more and more wealth at their expense. She had no use whatsoever for the arrogance of wealth. She was no poor church mouse, but her accumulation of modest wealth had never made her look down on those who had to struggle for their daily bread, because she had been there and done that. For her, what wealth she had accumulated made her realize that the system of capitalism was ill-suited to promote equality of opportunity, so she did all she could to always bend over and give people a hand up.

Among the grand and fashionable guests there was a sprinkling of the more important members of the literary world, a world Wayne preferred to avoid as he found most successful writers full of narcissism and self promotion, thinking that it was not luck or contacts that put them at the top of literary circles. Wayne knew from experience that those with recognizable family names did not have to look for an agent or publisher, all they had to do was offer a manuscript and it was accepted. That was one reason there was so much tripe in the marketplace. Often, success in writing was more marketing than talent, anyway. Also, nepotism was the bane of not only the literary world but the business and entertainment world as well. Just look at all the sons and daughters of movie stars and entertainment executives, directors, producers, etc. who are offered opportunities without the hard work others must go though for success. The world was full of talented individuals who never had a chance because they did not have the right connections. Thus, as Lynton meandered among the crowd, she felt that there were few people there with whom she would want to waste her time conversing. Lynton had actually taken the float plane one of Sue's relatives sent to pick them up, so they had avoided taking the ferry. These relatives thought Sue was too good to mingle with the common folk on the ferry. Lynton wore her usual off the rack clothing from an inexpensive shop, but her grace, poise and beauty made whatever she wore seem elegant.

Sue, in expensive clothing she felt obligated to wear, was adorned with fine jewellery that complimented her high-end designer apparel. To Sue's credit, she seemed uncomfortable with the ostentatiousness she felt compelled to display, so as not to create any disharmony with her relatives and executors of her estate.

Sensing her obvious uncomfortableness there, Lynton touched Sue's left arm gently and whispered. "I know how you feel. Isn't it horrible to have to endure being around so many people who think themselves special? The real special people are not here. They are in the dive pubs sipping cheap wine or beer rather than Dom Pérignon. They are in McDonald's rather than an upscale restaurant. These people here look with disdain on those who know that real wealth does not have to be displayed with ostentatious arrogance. Real wealth resides in the mind and heart, not in a bank where more money is stolen with the stroke of a pen than has ever been stolen by a desperate bandit seeking a few dollars to feed a hungry family or to feed a drug habit that society refuses to ameliorate by providing the help needed. I grow so weary of a society that talks about Christian charity, but displays none of it. Churches are locked up with empty pews while the homeless freeze on the sidewalks of despair caused by an economic system that has no heart or soul, a system that lacks a moral core."

Lynton and the Ladysmith Phantom

Taken with Lynton's discourse of rage against the machinery of capitalism in all its evil, Sue, gently grabbing Lynton's arm, said, "I am so glad I met you. You are everything Wayne said you are. You are a person who shines the bright light of hope where there is none."

"Sorry Sue, but affairs like this just drive me over the edge. I simply have little use for the privileged class, but, some of the privileged class are alright, I suppose. You are alright, because you see though the charade of vanity driven egotism, smugness and haughtiness."

Smiling, Sue said, "Let's get out of his den of pompousness. I want to take the late ferry home, where I can be comfortable with my new dear friend – you."

"Done," replied Lynton.

Ironically, the ferry (MC Coastal Inspiration) they took was the same one that Sue had taken when she saw the hooded man across from her and the child with its grieving mother. She instinctively led Lynton to the very seats where she and Dina had sat before. They sat quietly waiting for the ferry to leave port when a distinguished looking gentleman took a seat slightly to their right across from them.

There was only one word to describe the sun-kissed Grecian god-like creature of manliness in the seat opposite them. The word was "gorgeous." His eyes were the green of fresh dew glinting in the sunlight off a leaf of emerald. His lips were pale and thin and his nose slender and rounded. A prominent jaw curved gracefully and the strength of his muscular neck showed in the twining cords of muscle that shaped his entire body with strong sinewy arms, a firm chest and abdomen. He was an Adonis among the other men around them who each paled in comparison. One look and both women and men swooned at the sight of him no matter their sexual preferences. His expression was serious but not unkind. He had that salt and pepper look to his hair against his still youthful tight skin, but you knew he was in his mid 40's because of the air of confidence and assuredness. His voice, although uttering only one word, "hello," was as soft as wild honey dripping from a tree.

He smiled at Lynton and said, "I know you. I have read all fifteen Lynton books. Your pictures and descriptions by Wayne Frye do not do your beauty justice." He then looked directly at Sue and continued, "You also have a friend who rivals your exquisiteness."

Despite his boldness, neither woman was offended, because his manner was extremely respectful. After formal introductions he said to Sue, "I have heard of you, too. You live on a vast estate in Ladysmith high atop a mountain overlooking the ocean. That mountain has a very interesting history."

Curious, Lynton said, "And why not share some of that history with us? We are on a quest to find out more about the mountain and its somewhat sordid background."

Lynton and the Ladysmith Phantom

"Well, I have only a cursory knowledge, but there have been rumours of ghosts on that mountain. It goes back many years. Once, as a child, I was walking up the reservoir access road all alone, but, of course, did not go toward my left, as that is where the mist seems to always gather, and where no one ventures, because that is where the ghosts are rumoured to walk about. A young girl walked to the edge of the road, and I could not make her out well, because of the dense fog, but she seemed to be saying with her eyes, 'I am lonely, will you not come and play with me?' I was so scared I turned around and fled down the road, and that was the absolute last time I ever walked up that road again alone."

"I, as a young girl, played with a child in the forest named Elizabeth," said Sue.

Suddenly he looked extremely pale, and his breath caught itself. "What!" he exclaimed. "What did you say?"

"I said I played with a little girl named Elizabeth near that trail when I was little."

He pulled himself together almost instantly, though the colour did not come back to his face at once and his voice was not steady for a few seconds. "I beg your pardon," he apologized. "I am a bit discombobulated by your response. I thought you said something you could not possibly have said. You said that as a child you played with a little girl named Elizabeth."

"Yes," replied Sue. "She was so very fair, fairer than anyone I had ever seen; but when we played together she seemed like any other child. She was the first real playmate I ever had."

She told him about the first day they met and he seemed to be intensely interested, as if the little story quite fascinated him. It was only an episode, but it brought in the weirdness of Sue's childish fancies about the things hiding in the mist, and the mansion always being foreboding, and her fear to venture to where her father was killed. She told of Angus and the library, and Dina and her goodness and wise ways. It seemed dreadful to talk so much about oneself, but Sue felt so comfortable doing so to the handsome stranger named Derek Manly.

Lynton looked on as Sue continued unabated. It was curious to Lynton how this man had started out to tell what he knew, but was now listening intently to what Sue was saying. His eyes never diverted from staring intently at Sue.

His gaze became more pronounced as he said, "As a youth in Ladysmith, I lived right near where Pamela Anderson's grandmother lived. You know Pamela I am sure; the Hollywood personality. I used to walk up the hillside with friends where your estate is, because I was too afraid to take that road alone anymore. My mother admonished me to stay away from there, but you know how kids are. Telling them no just arouses their defiance. Still, as I walked up the road with my friends, I would shiver as I looked into that forest on the side of the mountain. Ah, but like all the other kids, I never ventured into the lower area over near what is now Thetis Road. We went to the mountaintop by using the access road to the reservoir where the city gets its water. We were very careful to skirt that area which always seems to be covered in a mist. We would often stand and listen to the creek that rumbles down the side of the mountain, and I swear that I heard crying near the creek, faint whimpers they were, faint whimpers that seemed to be pleading for some compassion. I always felt a tingle up and down my spine, because the cries seemed so pitiful, so pleading. I never saw the girl after that one time, only heard that whimpering. The odd thing is that my friends swore they heard nothing. They made fun of me to the point that I eventually, although hearing it often, denied that I did."

Lynton could sense he was still holding something back, when she said, "The girl's name, though. You found out her name."

Manly was visibly shaken, and his voice quivered as he replied, "Yes, I assume I know her name. You see, one day my friends and I walked up that road, and I looked over at the side where some long ago tossed away sand abutted the road. As always I looked over into the mist and heard that crying, the crying my friends never heard, I looked down and there it was in the sand, a plea spelled out in it, obviously written by a small finger. It read in scribbles: *Play with me. I am Elizabeth*. I called my friends over to show them. They laughed and kicked the sand away, saying that I was just trying to scare them by writing that the day before. I wish it had been true."

Lynton and the Ladysmith Phantom

Lynton said, "And what of an ominous dark figure? Have you ever encountered a dark, shadowy figure in that forest or anywhere else around the town?"

He turned white as chalk. His eyes and his mouth were frozen wide open in fearful expression of absolute stunned surprise, and although he was staring straight at Lynton he appeared not to notice her at all. Rather, his dazed look seemed to indicate he was drifting back in time, recalling a memory he did not want to recall, a memory that he had blotted out long ago, a memory that brought fear like a thug in the night in a dark alley.

"I never told anyone," he said as he seemed to snap back to reality. "How do you know about that dark, shadowy figure?"

They shared with Manly the tales of that dark figure the two of them had encountered, and to their surprise, he said, "I saw it a few times as a child over a period of about two weeks. I only saw it when I was alone, always alone." Then his breathing quickened, as he continued. "On a horrible day about thirty years ago, it trailed me hushed as the night, dancing between trees as the sunlight flickered. It melted into darkness with the arrival of dusk, until it blended and disappeared against the backdrop of nothingness. But then, as I lay in my bed looking out my window, it came back, causing within me a sense that it was longing, as if it desperately needed something. It was more an outline in the darkness, the fog. It was an echo of fear, an entity in search of something. What though I am not sure."

Lynton leaned forward and said, "You said a horrible day. My guess is that by horrible you mean something bad happened after you saw that figure, and my guess is also that after it happened you never saw it again? Am I right?"

"You are a very perceptive woman, Lynton," replied Manly.

"Keen perception has been both a curse and a blessing for me I am afraid. But go on. I am sure there is more to your story."

"You are right, as that very next morning my father and I woke, and we could not find my mother anywhere in the house. After an exhaustive search of our poor, dilapidated property, we looked all over town for her. Then we, along with our relatives and friends, combed all about the area but no one had seen or heard from her. Finally, we called the police, but it was absolutely futile. We never saw her again. The case went cold, and frankly, I assume they believed she had just run off with some other man."

"And, as I said, you never saw that dark figure again, right?" asked Lynton.

"Yes, never again, not ever."

Manly was not a man who had the air of talking about himself or sharing intimate details of his life, but before the three parted Lynton and Sue seemed to know him better than most. He was a painter and lived with his father when on Vancouver Island, but maintained an apartment in downtown Vancouver where he spent the majority of his time. As their conversation moved away from the ghost and dark figure, it became obvious that he was also a man of letters as a mere phrase of his would make a picture. Such few words made his father quite clear to Lynton and Sue. His father lived in the same house where his mother had disappeared so many years ago. The father had never remarried, and despite the noise of the major highway that the house now fronted he could not bear to sell it and move away. It was almost as if he expected his wife to show up there one day as if she had never disappeared. The father had actually ceased living, as the loss of his wife had sucked the life out of him. Manly only spoke of the house in such loving tones, and his description of his mother made one imagine her sitting under a great and ancient shade tree with the long, late-afternoon shadows stretching on the thick, green grass. That was the image both Lynton and Sue thought of when he said, "Will you come to tea under the big shade tree some afternoon when the late shadows are like velvet on the grass? That is perhaps the loveliest time."

They both eagerly agreed to visit. However, Lynton could not resist asking about the girl in the mist one more time. "And what of that girl? In all these years have you never wandered back up that road, searching for some clue about the girl, the crying?"

Shaking his head, he replied, "No, even at this age I am still afraid of what might be out there."

Lynton and the Ladysmith Phantom

As Derek and Sue walked down the ferry exit-way together while Lynton trailed behind, she was smiling with glee as she sensed the two had found grand simpatico by sharing their tales of woe. Manly probably did not even know that he put out his hand and gently touched Sue's arm, as one might touch a child to make it feel one wanted it to listen. Lynton heard Manly say to Sue in his deliberate voice, "You don't know how pleased I am that you have talked to me. I am glad someone else understands the mist of that abominable forest and the things that might be hidden in it. If you will come to tea, we will talk more about it. Of course, bring Lynton along, too."

"Indeed we will come," she answered. "I look forward to it."

The very next day he called, and Sue, along with Lynton, went over for tea and met his father, Wilton. They all sat under the large shade tree, despite the chilly time of the year. Its great branches spread out farther than Lynton had ever seen the branches of most trees spread before. They were gnarled and knotted and beautiful with age. Their shadows upon the grass were velvet, deep and soft. Such a tree could only have lived its life in such a well-cared for garden.

The high dim-coloured walls, with their curious low corner turns and the slight leafage of the nearby bush spread against the wall, and enclosed it as if embracing a lover not seen for a long time. But the shade tree itself seemed to have grown there in all its dignified loveliness of shadow to have once taken care of Manly's mother, who sat under it all those years, but now there was a drooping sadness to the tree, as if it longed for the return of she who brought so much comfort to the place that seemed stuck in perpetual melancholia.

The two men talked of Derek's mother, whose name seemed to fit their description of her perfectly. She was called Mary. They described her as clever, but very quite and not in the least bit old-fashioned. Her speech was exquisitely distinct, and when she would sit beneath the tree the branches seemed to bow in deference to her grace. She was tall for a woman, and her slenderness made her steps seem smooth and soft. She had a clear profile seemingly cut out of fine ivory and her head was beautifully shaped and set on a thin, delicate neck. Her every turn and movement was exquisite. She was quiet unaware of her loveliness, according to her son, who lovingly with trembling voice said, "She was not merely beautiful; she was beauty, beauty's very spirit moving about among us mortals. She was pure, perfect beauty of body, mind and spirit."

The love both men had for her was palpable. So distinct was it that both Lynton and Sue had moist eyes. Mary had been gone so long, but for the two men in her life it was like only yesterday she had disappeared, because for them she was the thread that held their lives together.

Lynton could see the feeling of belonging welling up in Sue, who had endured misery for so many years as a result of having no mother or father. It was obvious that Derek Manly made Sue feel a little as if, somehow, she belonged to someone now. She had always seemed so detached. She had not been miserable about it, and she had not complained to herself; she only accepted the detachment as part of her kind of life. However, now she had Lynton, who Wayne had brought into her life and finally the two Manly men, who made her feel so special.

It evidently made the two men happy to be near Sue, and as always, Lynton, ever the motherly type, kept Sue near her, and in some subtle, gentle way made her feel safe.

They sat under the tree until the long twilight deepened into shadow, which closed around them, and a nightingale that lived in the garden began to sing. It is a wonderful thing to sit quite still listening to a bird singing in the dark, and to dare to feel that while it sings it knows how your soul longs for peace.

They had been sitting listening for quite a long time, and the nightingale had just ceased and left the darkness in exquisite silence which fell suddenly but softly as the last note dropped, when Wilton Manly began to talk for the first time of what he called *the fear*. As he went on, and Derek joined in the talk, their meaning became a clear thing to the perceptive Lynton, and she knew that they were only talking quite simply of something they had often talked of before. They were respectful of *the fear* as most people in the town were, because they had heard so much about the evil that abounded in those woods that were off-limits to all who knew the story.

By *the fear* they meant that mysterious horror most people feel at the thought of passing out of the world they know into the one they don't know at all. They, and many others, felt that unknown world was in that mist on the mountainside. How quiet, how still it was inside the walls of the old garden, as the four sat under the main bough of the tree and talked. And what sweet night scents of falling leaves and winter calm were in every breath they drew. And how one's heart moved and lifted when the nightingale broke out again. The talk then continued about *the fear*.

"If someone besides me had seen or heard one little thing, if one's mortal being could catch one glimpse of light in the dark of that infernal forest," Derek Manly's low voice said out of the shadow near Sue, "*the fear* might be more recognizable."

"But you forget," interjected Sue, "I have seen her. I have played with her, though no words were ever spoken between us."

"Perhaps the whole mystery is as simple as this," said Lynton "that as there are tones of music too fine to be heard by the human ear, so there may be vibrations of light not to be seen by the human eyes of everyone, which may explain why only you two have communed with this little girl called Elizabeth. Form and colour, as well as sounds, can be just beyond earthly perception and yet as real as ourselves, as formed as ourselves, only existing in that other dimension. I believe I have the ability to perceive those things, which may explain why I also saw that dark shadowy figure on the ferry, just as Sue did."

There was an intenseness of hope in Lynton's rendition. She continued, "I think that somehow Elizabeth and that dark figure may be intertwined. Solve the mystery of one and you may well solve the mystery of the other. You, Derek, have sensed the little girl, and you also saw the dark figure outside your bedroom the very night before you and your father woke to find your mother gone. I think there may be a correlation."

There was an intense look on Wilton Manly's face. So intense was it that the highly perceptive Lynton said, "You know something you have never told, something that has just suddenly come back to you. Tell us."

Sighing heavily with a look of intense thoughtfulness, Wilton was very methodical in his response. "My mother once told me of a strong-looking young stranger with soft dark eyes who appeared out of the forest long ago, near where your father was killed Sue, and he married a boatman's daughter here in town. His wife, after about a year of marriage, saw a dark figure lurking about and told her husband about it. He went out to look for the figure, and he never came back into the house. He vanished. His wife had a son a few months later, as she had been pregnant. This son had an inquisitive nature just like his father, and she couldn't keep him away from that area near where the mist always lays about the forest. He claimed to often see a young girl in the mist, seemingly waving to him, but he never went to her, because of a feeling there was something lurking about within that was dangerous. When he was about sixteen he ran to his mother and said that there was a dark figure motioning at him outside their home, as if the figure wanted something from him. The figure he described was the same as his mother had seen before the father disappeared. She would not let him leave the house, not even for school. She kept him locked in the house for weeks. One night, when his mother was asleep, he slipped out by climbing into the attic and opening a window. He slid down a drainpipe. The police knew the mode he used to escape the locked house after a thorough investigation, but they found no trace of him and he was never seen again. However, there was a woman who used to live on Davis Road, a woman who most thought crazy; she swore that she had seen the boy walking with a dark figure toward the hillside and up the old access road where they paused and looked into the mist. She had discreetly followed them from a distance. Out of that mist came a little girl who seemed to be making a demand of the dark figure, almost ordering it to do something, but the dark figure seemed reluctant. The boy, seemingly hypnotized, went into that infernal forest, along with the little girl. They disappeared into the mist. Since the woman had always been what most referred to as 'touched,' no one took her seriously. What you

J. Wayne Frye

just said about a correlation between the two made me think of that story. I now believe it to be true. I believe you are right."

Lynton, who had dealt so often with the supernatural, was a mild sceptic, but she also had a healthy respect for the unknown in a world that always erected boundaries to keep control of people. Those in control did not want people asking questions. Religion, in particular, just wanted dedicated loyal adherents, not people with a genuinely inquiring mind. An inquiring mind was a danger to those in control, and the real purpose of religion was more about control than anything else. Keep people in constant fear of burning in hell, and it is much easier to control them, easier to make them dutifully bow before authority. Students were taught to accept what was in their text books as fact. Challenging a teacher was vehemently discouraged, because the real purpose of school was to programme workers for their corporate masters. Asking questions was discouraged, when it should be encouraged. This was the world far too many people were forced to accept, a world where those in control would provide the answers. This blind obedience to authority was why the poor actually lined up to cheer for the royal leeches of the world that pranced about in their finery while the very people who were cheering them lived a marginal existence. It was the reason demagogues and charlatans like that American narcissist President, Donald Trump, had the very people he held in disdain stand and wildly cheer him on without any understanding of how he was skilfully taking advantage of their gullibility.

Lynton said, "Again and again through all the ages we have been told the secrets of the gods and the wonders of the law as defined by those who believe all is simple to explain. We are slaves to a culture of ignorance." She then turned to Sue and said, "Like Wilton, you also have not shared all you know. Now is the time for you to get that something you have kept hidden off your chest."

Shaking her head, Sue replied to Lynton, "You are amazing. I have never seen anyone with your ability to ferret out information, your ability to know what someone is hiding and your ability to know what someone is thinking. You are right, of course. Yes, I have shared this with no one before tonight. I was asleep one night at my home on the mountainside. It was a dream, I assume. I found myself standing out on a hillside in moonlight softer and more exquisite than I had ever seen or known before. Perhaps I was still in my nightgown. I don't know. My feet were bare on the grass, and I wore something light and white which did not seem to touch me. If it touched me, I did not feel it. My bare feet did not feel the grass; they only knew it was beneath them. It was a low hill I stood on, and I was only on the side of it. And in spite of the thrilling beauty of the moon, all but the part I stood on melted into a soft, beautiful shadow, all below me and above me. But I did not turn to look about or ask myself about anything. You see the difficulty is that there are no earthly words to tell it! All my being was ecstasy; pure, light ecstasy! I was in sweet rapture! I did not look at the beauty of the night, the sky or the marvellous melting shadows. I was part of it all, one with it. I stopped and covered my face with my hands and tears wet my fingers. I reached over and touched a lone flower left on a bush, and I snatched it on the wintery cold day. Then a black cloud descended to cover the moon and blot out the light, turning everything dark. Oh, but what darkness it was. I've seen all kinds of darkness before, especially the kind that looks like an old fashioned photograph, everything a shade of grey. This wasn't like that. It was the darkness that robs you of your best sense and replaces it with a paralyzing fear. In this darkness I stood with muscles cramped unable to move. I only knew my eyes were still there, because I could feel myself blink, still instinctively moisturizing the organs I was trying to keep closed to still the sudden fear that had come upon me, but I could not. I couldn't hear anything either. I felt like prey in the utter blackness. The darkness there was cover for those that ventured out under its cover to join in some diabolical game practiced by those that scrounge for victims to satisfy evil intentions. Everything dissolved like it was never there at all, like the universe had not even begun. I felt more alone than ever before in my life. In the darkness I could not get a sense that anything was important at all except the darkness that wanted to envelop me. I wanted the dawn to come and kiss the land and remind this fickle heart that I was not the only one there – that there was a whole planet of people who live and love. But for that time all I had was a starless sky, and no light from the moon. I asked myself, where was the comforting light of that moon. Perhaps, it was like me – frightened, shivering, hiding behind a cloud in fear of the growing evil that was surrounding the forest. Then, suddenly, I realized where I was. I was where my father had died so many years before. I was overwhelmed with fear of what fate awaited me. It then was in the dream that a dark figure moved my way, until some small entity appeared, and seemed to stand between the dark shadow and me. Then, I suddenly felt pain in my neck. I awoke exhausted in my bed with sweat streaming down my forehead. I shivered in fear."

Lynton knew that was not the end. She said, "But the next morning, something made you realize it might not be just a dream. Right?"

Again shaking her head at Lynton's perceptiveness, she replied, "Of course not. There, lying on the floor was the flower I had plucked from the bush in my dream."

Chapter 4
Answers She has Sought for so Long

It is said that the spirits of buried men
Oft come to this wicked world again;
That the soft forest turf is often trod
By the tenants of tomb and sod;
That the midnight sea itself is swept
By those who have long beneath it slept.
And they say of this old, mossy wood
Whose tangled trees have for ages stood
That every knoll and dim lit glade
Is haunted by its restless shade.

"It was not a dream," Lynton said. "You came back for a reason, which I cannot presently discern; something may have interfered with the plans of that dark entity that has plagued this town now for so many years."

"Good night! Good night!" Wilton Manly said, and simply, with head bowed, got up and began to walk away. He turned back toward Lynton, and while Derek and Sue sat quietly he motioned, unseen by the two, for Lynton to join him.

She got up and said, "You two enjoy the cool night air, I'll join Mr. Manly inside."

Somehow Lynton realized, as had Wilton Manly, that Sue and Derek, although far apart age-wise, were developing a romantic attraction for one another and wanted to be alone. It made her think of Wayne, and how much she missed him. She hated his book signing trips almost as much as he did. She walked inside with Wilton, where they talked of *the fear* and how *the fear* had wrecked havoc in his and Derek's lives.

These four were trying to heap up for themselves proof that they might still be a chance to fight it, and somehow find an answer to the mystery of that dark figure and the little girl who made their homes in that misty area on the mountainside. For far too long the mystery of that forest had hung over the town, and soon Lynton would find out that these people were not the only ones affected. And, above all, it was obvious that Wilton Manly was delighted Lynton was going to join the fight against *the fear*, no matter what it might be. Lynton was a prolific fighter for those overwhelmed by adversity. It was simply in her nature.

Lynton and the Ladysmith Phantom

What Lynton had found out over the years was that all the things we think happen by chance and accident are often only part of the weaving of the scheme of life, chance and accident maybe, but not always. When you begin to suspect this and to watch closely, you also begin to see how trifles connect themselves with one another, and seem, in the end, to have led to a reason and a meaning, though we may not be clever enough to see it clearly. Nothing is truly accidental in most cases.

It may sound audacious, but Lynton decided that Angus's plethora of books about faiths and religions, books about philosophies and magic, books about what the world calls marvels, but which are not marvels at all, but only workings of the laws of the very often unseen and unheard that most people have not yet reasoned about or even accepted, were somehow hiding something important that he had just never revealed. Angus had read and studied books all his life before he began to read them with Sue, and Lynton talked about books together with him and her. They were by the fireplace in the library, fascinated as Angus sat in a high-backed chair, Dina standing by the fireplace while Lynton and Sue sat on the opposite side of the hearth on a sofa. Angus told them there is no such thing as chance.

What Lynton intended to say at first was merely that it was not by chance that she climbed to the top shelf in the library that afternoon and pushed aside the books hiding the old manuscript which told the real story of Dark Malcolm and

Elizabeth. It seemed like chance when it happened, but it was really the first step toward Lynton finding out the strange things that followed. The manuscript had been hidden for a reason she told Angus, who did not offer a reply.

Most people are bored by the prospect of life in a small town, howsoever picturesque the town might be. Of course, there was also the fact Sue's estate was isolated from the town in general, and there were no neighbours within at least a kilometre. The ancient stateliness was dull, but it was Sue's forced home as a result of a will that bound her there until her twenty fifth birthday. It was Sue having to live in this isolation which had made Lynton ponder on the reasons why a child would be forced to endure such a thing. Dina and Angus were apparently quite happy in their quiet way simply living there with Sue and the servants. Still, when Sue informed them that Wilton and Derek Manly were coming to visit that day, along with Lynton, they seemed unperturbed. When Derek and Wilton joined them in the library though, there was obvious consternation on Angus's and Dina's faces.

Of course, Angus was a bit shocked when he found out Lynton had come upon the manuscript which related the old story of Dark Malcolm and his child, Elizabeth. It had been pushed behind some volumes, and Lynton had taken it out, because it looked so old and yellow. She was mortified at what she read, and so would the others there be, who had now been joined by the

Manly's. It was a savage history of ferocious hate and barbarous reprisals. It had been a feud waged between two families with great tenacity. It was the story of Dark Malcolm who lived on the town side of the mountain and Blackie Redwood, who had an estate on the far side of the mountain. That was only part of it, but it was a gruesome part. Pages told of the bloody deeds they wrought on each other's houses. The one human passion of Dark Malcolm's life was his love for his little daughter. She had brown eyes and brown hair, and those who most loved her called her Lizzie. Blackie Redwood was apparently richer than Malcolm, and therefore could more easily work his cruel will. He knew well of Malcolm's worship of his child, and laid plans to kidnap her for some unknown reason. Dark Malcolm, coming back to his home after a ride to Duncan, which was 25 kilometres away, found that Elizabeth had been carried away, and unspeakable terror of what fate would befall her was raging about within him. Dark Malcolm and his henchmen rushed forth into the night. They were a band of madmen in their black despair. How they tore through the night and found an unguarded weak spot in the walls around Blackie's estate. Then, they fought their way through and over the wall, leaving countless dead bodies in the path. By strange chance Malcolm came upon Elizabeth, craftily set to playing hide-and-seek with a child of Blackie's so that she might not cry out and betray her presence; but already mortally wounded, Malcolm caught

Blackie's daughter and with utter cruelty, he contemplated slaying her with his hunting knife, slitting her throat as retribution for the kidnapping of Malcolm's daughter, but he could not do it. Seeing that he was the last man standing after all his men had been killed in the raid, he realized his daughter would suffer a cruel fate from Blackie Redwood as revenge. He took his daughter to his bleeding breast, and stabbed her in the back to protect her from a fate he considered worse than death. He, falling dead as he held her body against his breast, with her long brown hair streaming over it, embraced her lovingly. That was long before the town of Ladysmith was even built. Blackie's estate was shrouded in overgrowth today as the forest reclaimed it. There was little trace of it now, save the stern stone walls which once surrounded the stately home. Where Blackie went absolutely no one knew, but Dark Malcolm's stately place also remained deserted for many years, until Sue's parents, despite rumours of it being haunted, bought it with no concern whatsoever in regards to the rumours of ghosts and ghouls being about.

Lynton was now ready to ask a question that demanded a definitive answer. She looked directly at Angus and said, "You have read the manuscript, so don't look surprised. I want to know, as I am sure Sue does, why you never shared this information with her. I assume it had nothing to do with her father and mother, so is there a valid reason why you would not tell her about this? You have shared all these books. Why have you never told her of Elizabeth, Blackie and Malcolm?"

"Why would I share such a cruel story with someone I revered so dearly? The tale of Blackie Redwood and Dark Malcolm is filled with anguish. I saw no need to share it with her."

Lynton said, "But we both know that Sue played with Elizabeth, don't we?"

He sighed and looked over at Dina, standing by the hearth. "I never saw any little girl, nor did Dina?"

"Just because you could not see her does not mean she was not there. Some people are not as psychically attuned as others." Then Lynton stroked the old manuscript with her hand questioningly. "Honestly, did this fall at the back by accident, or did you hide it?"

"I hid it," he answered. "It was no tale for a young thing to read. I have hidden many from her. She was always poking about, and I saw no reason to scare an impressionable young girl with such horrors."

Lynton very pointedly said, "She is no wee child any longer! It is time for her to know how her father really died. It was no hunting accident was it?"

Surprised as usual by Lynton's perceptiveness, Sue interjected with deep intensity, "Lynton! You are saying my dad was not killed in a hunting accident? It can't be true."

Lynton looked over at Dina and said, "Tell her the truth about that day her father died, and then tell her about the dark figure you saw the night her mother died."

Floored by all that Lynton discerned from research she had done, Dina looked over at Angus, without understanding that what Lynton knew was more conjecture than hard facts. She said, "No one was really sure what happened, but it seemed prudent to simply say it was an accident; that he had stepped in a gofer hole and lost his balance. The gun was loaded and went off, killing him instantly."

"But what really happened was that he was terribly frightened by something that day. Am I right?" interjected Lynton.

"Yes, you see, he fell behind the rest of the hunting party and they never really missed him until the shot was heard. He did not die instantly as everyone agreed to say." She then looked sympathetically at Sue and continued, "Rather, as he lay mortally wounded, with half his face blown away, he kept muttering something through what was left of his lips about a small girl who came at him from the forest and reached out with a cold, calculating hand, tilted his gun upward and pulled the trigger. He was delirious and dying, so it was assumed he was hallucinating." She then looked pathetically at Sue, almost pleading with her. "Forgive me my dear girl. I never wanted to burden you with this. There is so much that no one has ever been able to answer. It just seemed prudent to spare you the pain. You have suffered so much."

J. Wayne Frye

Very determined, Sue replied "A lie causes more pain than the truth. Do not lie anymore. This is the time to lay it all out in an untarnished fashion."

"You are right of course, but there was so much chaos that day we all fell victim to expediency. Nobody saw that figure in the forest but your father, and you know how sensitive your relatives are about any impropriety that might tarnish the precious family name they all think is so revered. They thought it was just a figment of his imagination, but later on I knew it was more than that, much more."

Lynton said, "You saw a dark figure in the back of that bedroom when Sue's mother died, because I found your account in another volume that had been hidden in the library stacks, but you do not think it was the ghost of Sue's father come to wait lovingly for his wife. That is what you wish it was, but you know different. You were surprised when you saw it, but my guess is you were more psychically attuned that night, because of the unusual circumstances. You see, certain circumstances in certain situations actually heighten our psychic powers. I would say that what you saw that night, for lack of a better word, was transcendental, something that had managed to come from another realm. That entity is, in my humble opinion, perhaps none other than Blackie Redwood, but I am not sure it is a ghost. I think it might be something much more than a mere ghost, but I will explore that at a later time."

Overwhelmed by Lynton's perceptive powers, all there stared in disbelief as she turned to Sue and said, "You played with a child as a youth, but the two of you never spoke did you?"

"No, never."

Lynton stood, walked deliberately over to the fireplace, sighed, turned and said to Sue, "Tell us about your interaction with that child called Elizabeth."

"She was forlorn a lot of the time. I would speak with her, but she would never reply verbally, only by symbolic gestures that I grew to understand. She would go frolicking gaily about, even smiling, as if her only happiness was with me. Still, there was something strange as the bloody spot over her heart seemed to renew itself on occasion. It would be clean for a long, long while, but always came back periodically, seemingly fresh with blood."

Looking out the window down at the area where Sues' father's body was brought home, Lynton did not turn toward her as she, still gazing out the window, said "That dark figure that came at you all those years ago from the misty forest, are you sure that it had nefarious intentions toward you?"

"Yes, I assume so," replied Sue.

Lynton turned, looking all about the room, then directly at Sue, as she said "So it was obvious the thing, whatever it was, actually knew the little girl, Elizabeth."

"Yes."

J. Wayne Frye

"But Elizabeth had no fear of it? In fact, it was more like the thing feared her?"

Looking a bit perplexed as if in deep thought about the question, Sue replied, "You know what? I never thought about it before, but yes – yes. It was in awe of her. What does it mean?"

Lynton, as always, cautious about revealing her thoughts before having solid, verifiable proof said, "I am only forming the nucleus of a theory at this point. I need more information to be sure what I am postulating could be fact."

All there could scarcely look away from Lynton, seemingly waiting for the next revelation from her. She, still standing by the window, pointed in the distance to the left. "There, near the area where your father was killed is where you first saw Elizabeth. Am I right?"

"Yes, it was near where my father died, but we never went past the hilly area, never ventured into the glade. Everyone avoided that, for there is a feeling you get as you near that area, a feeling that there is something lurking there, something that is evil."

Lynton was very deliberate in her speech now. "That is where you played with Elizabeth the first time, when Dina and Angus could not see her?"

"Yes."

"Will you take me there tomorrow?" said Lynton with steely confidence. "I could go by myself, but I think it better you go with me, because I may have some pertinent questions that can be better answered in that place."

"Would you like to go early in the morning? The mist is more likely to be there then, as it was that day. It is incredibly mysterious, but despite that it is, without doubt, equivalently beautiful at the same time."

"Was that the time of the day you first saw her? Lynton asked.

"Yes, in the morning."

Wilton and Derek Manly had been totally silent through the entire evening, sitting with intense interest at what was being said by those present, but suddenly Wilton said, "Is this at all related to the disappearance of my wife?"

Lynton very sympathetically replied, "I am not 100% sure, but I think it is, yes. I think it is related to the other two disappearances that occurred after Sue saw that dark figure. Sue, I believe, has psychic powers she is unaware of. And I also believe your son has them, too. Be patient with me, because I do not want to offer hope where there is none. That is why I must wait before making some definitive conclusions based upon my experience and what few facts I have gathered here in Ladysmith." She then looked over at Sue, continuing, "You are more central to this then you may imagine, and I do not want to frighten you, but be very vigilant in all you do, because I feel you may be in danger. Danger of what, danger where, danger how; I am unable to say with any certainty, but there is evil lurking about, evil that has been here many, many years, and I am going to do more research, but I think, believe it or not, that your father's and mother's deaths and all the other disappearances are related. I do not want to give you any hope that anyone is alive, but I can give you hope that we may well arrive at some answers that might offer an explanation of what happened to all those people, and I believe to many more. I have a puzzled feeling about Elizabeth. This afternoon I found an old book in the Ladysmith Library that was gathering dust on a high shelf in the rare book reading room. Obviously, it had been there many years, and just as obviously ignored. It was the history of the feud between Blackie Redwood and Dark Malcolm. Does that mean you played with a ghost? No, as it could have been someone with the same name, but it appears the Redwood family dispersed, or completely disappeared after the raid on Blackie's place. And why would there be no record of any girl named Elizabeth anywhere around here at the time you met her? Then there is the mystery of her mother. From what I have found, it appears that her mother, on Elizabeth's fourth birthday had a terrible accident. She fell from a balcony and nearly died before they could get her back inside and call a physician. She proclaimed as she lay nearly dying that she was the victim of foul play. She declared that she felt a hand push her over the balcony railing as she stood there looking out over the estate. The entire staff was questioned but to no avail. Afterward, Dark Malcolm became both mother and father to Elizabeth when her mother eventually did die in unusual circumstances."

"Poor little soul, with the blood pouring from her heart and her brown hair spread over her dead father's breast in the end!" stated Sue.

"I wonder if it was exactly over her heart?" offered Lynton.

"There was a little mark far to the left. The heart is actually in the middle of the chest. So no, it was not exactly over the heart."

Lynton interjected, "And what of her back? Was there a definitive stab mark back there?

"Yes, as far as I could discern."

Lynton then asked, "Did she always wear the same clothes?"

"Oh yes!"

"Was she usually aware of the blood stain?"

"She looked at it, but only in a cursory way, and she seemed, after our first meeting, to be unperturbed about it."

Lynton looked again at Angus and Dina. It was a pointed look they returned. It was absorbed, strange and quizzical, as Lynton said, "You have seen Elizabeth, not every time, but on occasion."

Nodding both their heads in agreement, it was Angus who said, "We knew what was going on, but feared alarming Sue. We feared her reaction if we told her she was playing with a ghost."

Lynton took a deep breath and said, "Elizabeth may not be a ghost. There are all kinds of entities about, not every one is a ghost. It is too early for me to say for sure, but this is a most perplexing situation, and I believe a stroll with Sue there tomorrow may help with some answers."

Lynton and the Ladysmith Phantom

The area wore its most mysterious look when Lynton and Sue stood looking down the hillside the next day. It had hidden itself in the soft hews of a swathing mist. Only here and there dark trees showed themselves above it, and now and then the whiteness thinned or broke and drifted.

Sue had never known that there could be such a feeling of genuine companionship until Lynton arrived into her life, but she was really surprised when Derek showed up and said, "I know I am not invited, but I do not think two women should go alone into the infernal area where so much evil appears to be lurking."

It was not necessary for Lynton to say anything; because she knew the real reason Derek Manly was there. He had almost instantly fallen for Sue. Lynton said nothing to him, just smiled and started walking. Sue and Derek followed, whispering in quiet voices which seemed to be made quieter by the mist. The area was dark and thickly grown over with dead heather and flowerless broom. As they moved ever forward, the mist grew thicker. There were streams that rushed and made guiding sounds which were sometimes loud whispers and sometimes singing babbles. The damp, sweet scent of moss was in their nostrils, as they descended ever downward.

"There is a sort of unearthly loveliness in it all," said Derek.

"I believe there are ghosts here," Sue offered. "They might be those the mist hides, because they like to be hidden. The mist is their blanket."

"You would not be afraid if you met one of them?" asked Derek.

"No. I am sure of that. I should feel that it was afraid of me more than I of it, and, if it could speak, it might tell me things I want to know."

"What do you want to know?" Lynton asked.

"I want to know there is no reason to be afraid. So many people have been afraid for so long. All of my life I have lived in fear of some unidentifiable thing, and I am tired of it."

Lynton very stoically said, "Being afraid is what sometimes keeps us alive, but it can also make us into the living dead. Life shrinks or expands in proportion to one's courage. Fear defeats more people than any other thing in the world. Fear is pain arising from the anticipation of evil, because we are conditioned by a world that wants us to live in fear: fear of losing a job, fear of being a failure, fear of the moneyed and privileged classes, fear of the government and the authorities that are sent out to keep us in line, fear of saying or doing the wrong thing that will lead to being ostracized, fear of that supposedly all-powerful God up in the sky that loves us so much but is always watching us and knows all our thoughts and desires that he will punish us for, fear of the devil in the bowels of the earth where if we are not good little boys and girls we will go to live among those devils with pitchforks to prod us for all eternity in retribution for our ill thoughts and deeds. Fear is what keeps the many enslaved to the few."

How, thought Derek and Sue, could one little Filipino mite of a girl be so imbued with such great depth of understanding about the way the world worked? Like so many others, they were mesmerized by the dynamic dynamo.

They brushed through the winter leafless and flowerless heather and broom, as the mist wavered and sometimes lifted opening up mystic vistas only to veil them again a few seconds later. The sun tried to break through, and as a result, sometimes they walked bathed in a golden haze.

They were silent, seemingly waiting anxiously for something to appear or for some sound to break through the thick mist. Now and then Sue glanced sidewise at Derek, as they made their soundless way through the thick moss-covered trees. He looked so strong and handsome. His tall body was so fine, his shoulders so broad and so splendid! As he tramped beside Sue he was thinking deeply, and he knew he need not talk to her. He knew she could feel his affection.

Suddenly, there came from far in the distance the sound of flapping wings. The sound was drawing nearer.

"Perhaps it is a bird," offered Sue.

"It is not a bird," replied Lynton. "It is something more ominous than just a bird."

The mist was clearing, and it floated about like a thin veil through which one could see objects. At a short distance above they saw something, a dark shadow moving across the sky. It appeared to be a huge bat. Why was it out in the daytime all wondered? It passed out of sight and disappeared into the mist.

Seeing that Sue was tiring, Derek said, "She is tired Lynton, let's stop here by the rocks and rest. Derek then bent down, placed a handkerchief over the rock, took Sue's hand and guided her to sit on the rock. Lynton, smiling, was not perturbed by Derek's neglect of gentlemanliness toward her, as she was thrilled to see a romance developing between the two. It would be the same May-December romance she and Wayne shared.

Derek turned to Lynton, and said, "That was a bat, right?"

"Maybe," replied Lynton, as the mist seemed to be clearing. "We should head back now. We have accomplished more than you realize."

"What do you mean?" asked Derek.

"I cannot give you a definitive answer yet, but there are more than mere ghosts here I believe, much more, and if I am right, a ghost would be a blessing. I have to do some research before I can give you a more cogent explanation of that thing in the sky."

When they got back to the library, an anxious Angus greeted Lynton. "Will you come with me, all of you?" he said. It was obvious he had something he wanted to share, something terribly important. "It is a sad thing you have to hear."

Ever perceptive, Lynton said, "Someone has disappeared."

Angus stood still and watched her in total disbelief. "How do you know?"

"Well, chalk it up to experience. Who was it?" replied Lynton.

"Supposedly a man named Harry Stammer, who was staying at the only hotel in town. He was here on business."

Lynton said, "And how are you sure he disappeared?"

"Well, it seems that last night he came into the hotel manager's office very upset. He said there was a dark figure following him around the hotel and to a local restaurant where it waited for him to finish his evening meal, seeming to signal to him for some reason. He pointed outside the office at an open space and said, 'See, there the infernal thing is right now.' The manager saw nothing, no one at all outside. The man became irate, went outside and moved quickly toward the area where he said the dark figure was. The man was waving his hands wildly, until he finally turned and ran back toward his room. Within maybe one minute he called the front desk and screamed uncontrollably, 'It's here; it has come for me. It is going to take me. Help me! Help me!' The manager ran to the room. The door was open and inside it appeared there had been a struggle. He immediately called the RCMP, but after an exhaustive search and investigation no sign of the man could be found. They are still scouring the town trying to find him."

Everyone gazed toward Lynton as if pleading for help. Lynton looked directly at Sue and said, "You have always had part of the answer, as have a few others, including Angus and Dina. Tell me about something unusual from your early childhood, something that really surprised you, even may have caused you great fear. It may have been one time or many when someone was able to tell you how you were different. Tell me with complete candour."

Shaking her head from left to right and then back, Sue said, "You are so amazing. When I was three, I had a nurse who actually left employment here after she said to me that I had the eyes which *SAW*. It was only the saying of an old foolish nurse I thought. She said to me, 'It is more curse than gift, and I shall not be around one with that accursed power.' Later I began to believe I had a sight that others did not have, because I saw things others did not."

"I know the feeling Sue, and it is definitely both a curse and a blessing, but," and then Lynton looked over at Angus and Dina as she continued, "these two know more than they have ever been willing to share."

Angus and Dina hung their heads, almost in shame. Angus took a deep breath and said, "We did not see the girl, Elizabeth, but we did know of the tales. We had always hidden our knowledge because we were afraid it might frighten Sue to be told. She was not a strong child. We kept the secret because of her relatives who would not believe, and also who would perhaps arrange to get us fired. We had fears of what might be done with doctors and severe efforts to obliterate from

Sue what her relatives would have called mindless nonsense."

Lynton interjected, "It has taken man eons to reach the point where he is beginning to know that in every stock and stone in his path may lie hidden some power he has not yet dreamed of. He has learned that distance can be conquered, space can be explored, motion chained and utilized; but he, the one conscious force, has never yet begun to suspect that of all others he may be the one as yet the least explored. How do we know that there does not lie in each of us a wholly natural but, so far, dormant power of sight, a power to see what has been called the unseen through all the ages whose sightlessness has made them dark? Who knows when the shadow around us may begin to clear? Who knows what you have kept hidden for years, but are now going to share."

Almost pensively, Angus said, "When your mother was about to bring you into the world she was listening to someone or something outside in the forest calling to her. She would sit for hours on the balcony of her bedroom enthralled by something in that forest. She would, on occasion, whisper to herself, 'it killed him.' Neither of us ever asked her what she meant, for we assumed she was in almost constant delirium from the loss of her husband, whom she loved so dearly. At night we would sit with her as she, wrapped in a blanket under stars which seemed to be listening to her silence, stared constantly into that infernal mist. She had lost the will to live, lost all hope."

Dina interrupted. "I did see that mother and child on the ferry, but I knew they were not living things, nor was the thing sitting across from us. When the poor mother struggled with grief, you looked so slight and small my dear Sue. Then, a far look in your eyes made me begin to watch you out of the corners of my eyes. You were so sorry for the poor woman that you could not look away from her, and something in your face touched and puzzled me. There is a profound goodness in you Sue. That night when you spoke quite naturally of the child, never doubting that I had seen it, I suddenly began to suspect you had the same gift that Angus and I sometimes have. I had been reading and thinking many things new to me. I did not know what I believed. But you spoke so simply, and I knew you were speaking the truth. You had also spoken previously of Elizabeth. That startled me because not long before I had been told the tale of *the fear*. I knew you had never heard the story before. And yet you were telling me that you had played with that child – that thing."

Lynton interjected, "To some it would mean something; to some it would mean nothing. To those with extra sight, it has a meaning that opens wide windows into the light of understanding. That would be quite enough, even if the rest thought it only the weird fancy of a silly girl who had lived alone and given rein to her silliest imaginings. Today, you have given Sue a new opening to answers she has sought for so long."

Chapter 5
There is Evil About

Up the airy mountain,
Down the brushy glen
Her father dared to go a-hunting,
For he was brave and bold among men.
But he knew not what waited that day,
Trooping off with all the party together;
Green jacket, red cap
And white owl's feather!

Down along the rocky plain
Some resident evil made its home.
It lived off others pain,
With blood boiling into foam.
Spying from the misty reeds

Lynton and the Ladysmith Phantom

Off the black mountain-lake,
With sinister intentions it rose
To make evil wide awake.

In the high hill-top home,
The wife with shudders sits.
She knows there is evil below.
She's nigh lost her wits,
With worrisome stares into the mists.
Though not religious, she makes crosses,
For she fears the evil below
That is as dark as black roses.

There down the hillside
On a cold starry night
She sees the wings in the distance,
Blotting out the moon light
By the craggy hillside
Through the mosses bare.
She sees the knotty thorn trees,
And she knows evil lurks there.

Why is her husband so daring,
While she stares in fright?
She wearies of sharp thorns
That penetrate her dreams at night.
The day is darkening round her.
The wild winds coldly blow,
As torrents of evil begin to stir,
And cannot let good blood go.

The giant trees are bending;

J. Wayne Frye

Lynton and the Ladysmith Phantom

Their bare boughs weighed so low.
The storm is fast descending,
And she realizes the power of her foe.
Clouds beyond clouds above her,
Wastes beyond wastes below,
But mesmerized she cannot stir.
The feeling of doom she cannot let go.

Her strong enchantments failing,
Her towers of fear in wreck,
Her mouth sensing the taste of death's poisons,
And the teeth of evil seem at her neck.
The bat of grey air and darkness
Begins to shrill and cry:
"I am a bloody slayer,
And I shall dance as you die."

The shrill sound would not fade,
As that infernal bat soared,
And darkness fell across the glade.
Hear the shrill cry from high:
"I am queen of air and darkness.
'Tis truth of doom you cannot defy.
You shall sense life's starkness,
And you will in your grave soon lie."

It is probable that everybody who is at all a dreamer has had at least one experience of an event or a sequence of circumstances which have come to the mind in sleep being subsequently realized in the material world. It is actually perfectly normal that this fulfilment happens on occasion, since our dreams are, as a rule, concerned with people who we know and places with which we are familiar, such as might very naturally occur in the awake and day lit world. True, these dreams are often broken into by some absurd and fantastic incident, which puts them out of court in regard to their subsequent fulfilment, but on the mere calculation of chances it does not appear in the least unlikely that a dream imagined by anyone who dreams, as we all do, should not occasionally come true. It was this knowledge that allowed Lynton to ask Dina, who had been a loyal companion to Sue's mother, a question that would lay the foundation for what would be a revelation of monumental proportions. She, looking with intensity into Dina's eyes, said with her soft, sympathetic voice, "You must now tell us all you know, all that you have kept hidden for so many years. Bare all, because I am sure that I am coming to a conclusion that you will validate, though you might not understand it at present."

It was then that Dina, who, at the age of 16, went to work for Sue's mother, Clara, related the story of how Clara had a certain friend living abroad, who, in the day of computer infancy, was technologically astute enough to communicate by the device with Sue's mom almost every day. Clara delighted in hearing from the friend. Thus, when fourteen days or thereabouts elapsed since she last heard from him, her mind, probably either consciously or subconsciously, was filling with worry about him. One night she dreamed that as

J. Wayne Frye

she was going upstairs just before dinner she heard something she rarely heard, the sound of a knock on the front door just at the end of the day when night was slowly creeping in as the daylight faded and the quarter moon appeared. The sound diverted her attention downstairs, where there, an exhausted looking postman was delivering to one of the maids a rare, for that day and age, special delivery letter from the very person of whom she was worried. As the mailman left, the maid closed the door and looked up at the mistress of the house, who had come to the bottom of the stairs. She extended her hand, which contained the envelope from the friend whose name was Darren McCloud. Sue's mother nervously took it from her. Thereafter, the extraordinarily fantastical entered into the picture, for upon opening the letter, she found inside the ace-of-spades, and scribbled across it in the well-known handwriting of her friend was the words, *"I am sending you this for a reason I shall explain upon my arrival in a week."* It was then that Sue's mom looked out the window and saw a dark figure in the front yard. It simply raised its left hand in a waving, almost pleading motion. She looked up at the quarter moon and observed a bat fluttering about. She then turned her attention back to the dark figure, but it was gone, seemingly disappearing into thin air.

The next day as she sat in the parlour with her husband, who had drifted off to sleep, she heard a knock on the door. She quickly got up and waved the maid off as she moved toward the door, saying, "I will answer it." There was a postman with a special delivery letter. Remembering her dream, she tepidly opened it. It did not contain the ace of spades, but it said that Darren would be arriving for a visit the following week. Had it included the aforementioned ace of spades, she might have, no doubt, attached more weight to the matter as it related to the dream. However, she, consciously or subconsciously, expected a letter from him, per the dream.

This strange occurrence, according to Dina, preyed upon Clara's mind a long time, as the two of them had always communicated by computer. Time went by slowly and each day after the week she expected his arrival. However, not only did he not arrive, but she never saw or heard from him again. He seemed to have simply dropped off the face of the earth. However, she did, one day, find in the shrubbery to the left of the door a tattered ace-of-spades. She never told anyone about it out of fear people would think she was crazy. Darren's family was shocked about his disappearance as was Clara.

Clara then related to Dina the strange circumstances of a dream she had experienced for years. She was a young unmarried girl when a certain dream first came to her about being placed down at the door of a huge house, where, she understood, she was going to stay for awhile. The servant who opened the door told her that tea was being served in the garden, and led her through a low dark-panelled hall with a large open fireplace on to a cheerful green lawn set round with flower beds. There were grouped about the tea-table a small party of very unusual looking people, all seemingly very dark and sombre, almost zombie-like. They were all strangers to her, including one who was a fellow named Blackie, clearly the house's owner, and he introduced her to many of the aforementioned unusual guests. She was somewhat astonished to find herself there, for the man in question, Blackie, was not known to her, and she rather disliked him almost instantly. The afternoon was very hot, and an intolerable oppression reigned. On the far side of the lawn ran a red-brick wall, with an iron gate in its centre. It seemed more fortification than wall. They sat in the shadow of the huge house, which appeared to actually be more like a castle than a home, and opposite a row of long windows, inside which she could see a table with a cloth laid upon it, glimmering with glass, fine china and polished silver utensils. This garden front of the house was very long, and at one end of it, which solidified her view that it was more castle than house, stood a tower of three stories, which looked to her much older than the rest of the building. Before long, Blackie introduced a woman he called mother, but Clara knew she was not really his mother. She said to him with evil twinkling eyes, "Blackie will show you to your room. You have been given the room in the tower." A sinister grin greased her lips and she continued, "You'll find it delightful."

Lynton and the Ladysmith Phantom

Quite inexplicably her heart sank at those words. She felt as if she had known that she should have the room in the tower, and that it contained something dreadful. Blackie instantly got up, and she understood that she had to follow him. In silence they passed through the hall, and mounted a great oak staircase and arrived at a small landing with two doors set in it. He pushed one of these open for Clara to enter, and without coming in himself, closed it after her. Then she knew that her conjecture had been right: there was something awful in the room, but she still lay down and drifted off to sleep. With the terror of a nightmare growing swiftly and enveloping her, she awoke in a spasm of terror.

Now that dream or variations on it occurred to her intermittently over the years. Most often it came in exactly the same form, the arrival, the tea laid out on the lawn, the deadly silence succeeded by those two horrific sentences, mounting the stairs with Blackie up to the room in the tower where horror dwelt, and it always came to a close in the nightmare of terror about that which was in the room, though she never saw what it was. It was more feeling than anything else, but she always found herself weak and exhausted the entire next day. At other times she experienced variations on this same theme. Occasionally, for instance, she would be sitting at dinner in the dining-room, but wherever she was, there was the same silence, the same sense of dreadful oppression and foreboding. And the silence she

J. Wayne Frye

knew would always be broken by Blackie's supposed mother saying, "Blackie will show you to your room. I have given you the room in the tower." Upon which (this was invariable) she had to dutifully follow Blackie up the elaborate oak staircase and enter the place that she dreaded more and more each time that she visited it in her sleep. Or, sometimes she would find herself playing cards and having an ace-of-spades in her hand. There was silence in a barely lit drawing-room that gave a feeling of dread. What game she was playing she had no idea; what she always remembered, with a sense of horribly miserable anticipation, was that soon Blackie's mother would get up and say to her the same thing that was always said. This drawing-room where she played cards was always in near darkness, and the rest of the house was always full of dusk and shadows. In fact, the shadows seemed to be moving all about. And she never really seemed to be awake. The card designs were strange: there were no red suits, but all were black, and among them there were certain cards which were black all over. She hated and dreaded those cards, and that terrible room.

According to Dina, she indicated that as this dream continued to recur Clara got to know the greater part of the house. There was a strange room beyond the drawing-room at the end of a passage with a green door. It was always very dark there, and as she went there she passed someone she could not see very well in the doorway coming out. She felt like she knew the person. Curious developments, too, took place in the characters that peopled the dream. Blackie's supposed mom, for instance, who, when Clara first saw her, had been black-haired, became grey, and instead of rising briskly, as she had done at first, she got up very feebly, as if the strength was leaving her limbs. Blackie also sometimes became a rather ill-looking man, with a short brown moustache that had specks of grey.

Then it so happened that Clara's dream ceased for almost six months, until one night after this interval she again found herself being shown out onto the lawn for tea, and Blackie's mother was not there, while the others were all dressed in black. At once she guessed the reason, and her heart leaped at the thought that perhaps this time she should not have to sleep in the room in the tower, and though all there usually sat in silence, on this occasion two of the guests talked and laughed. But even then matters were not altogether comfortable, for no one else spoke, but they all looked secretly at each other. And soon the stream of staring ran dry, and gradually an apprehension worse than anything she had previously known gained on her as darkness seemed to engulf the entire house. Suddenly a voice which she knew well broke the stillness, the voice of Blackie's mother, saying, "Blackie will show you to your room. I have given you the room in the tower." It seemed to come from near the gate in the red-brick wall that bounded the lawn, and looking up, she saw that the grass outside was sown thick with gravestones. A curious greyish light shone from them, and she could read the lettering on the grave nearest her, and it was, "In devilish memory of Soirée McKenzie." Clara had never known her name until then, but obviously it was the woman who always said those faithful words to her who had died, but was still talking to her from the grave. And as usual, Blackie got up, and again she followed him through the hall and up the staircase. On this occasion it was darker than usual, and when she passed into the room in the tower she could only just see the furniture, the position of which was already familiar to her. Also, there was a dreadful odour of decay in the room. She looked at Blackie, who seemed delighted that she had to again endure that infernal room. He left. She, frightful, but too tired to fight off sleep, fell into a deep slumber. She awoke screaming in her own bed at home, with an intense pain in her neck.

The dream, with such variations and developments as mentioned, went on at intervals for many years. Sometimes she would dream it two or three nights in succession, but with occasional respites that lasted, as mentioned previously, for up to three months. It had, as is plain, something nightmarish about it, since it always ended in the same appalling terror, which far from getting less, seemed to gather fresh fear every time that she experienced it, but she could never really remember what caused the terror. The characters got more sombre and evil looking with each visit, and she never in the dream, after Soirée had apparently died, set eyes on her again. But it was always her voice that told her that the room in the tower was prepared for her, and whether it was tea out on the lawn, or the scene was laid in one of the rooms overlooking it, she could always see Soirée's gravestone standing just outside the gate. Then, the dreams simply stopped, but she never knew why. She thought that perhaps it was because of a malady which afflicted her. The malady had progressed gradually, as she had a slight swelling on her neck area that no doctor could explain. The swelling appeared, disappeared and then reappeared at three month intervals. However, there was an unusual feeling that came over her, a feeling that she could not shake, a feeling that there was doom waiting. Yet, she and her husband were happy, despite this feeling. Then one day they set off about five in the afternoon, after a thoroughly delightful day, for a walk into the forest. They walked and walked, enjoying the long summer day. As they began the trek back home, the weather became very stagnant and oppressive, and they both felt that indefinable sense of ominous apprehension as they heard the roar of thunder in the distance. Suddenly, before them was an old, withered and white-haired man standing by a tree. But in spite of the evident feebleness of body, a dreadful exuberance and vitality shone through the envelope of flesh, exuberance wholly malign, a vitality that foamed and frothed with unimaginable evil. Evil beamed from the narrow, leering eyes; it showed in the sinisterly curved demon-like mouth. The whole face was imbued with some secret and appalling malignancy; the hands seemed to be shaking with suppressed and nameless desires, but they did not appear old. Rather they appeared young and unlined. He laughed at them and said, "I will have you both." That was when time seemed to be suspended and the two of them felt frozen in place with eyes closed, bringing intense darkness all about, and in what seemed the blink of an eye they appeared to wake from a deep sleep. They saw the old man walking into the thick forest, and he seemed to slowly dissipate before their eyes. Then they looked behind them and there stood that infernal dark figure maybe fifty metres away, and just as it had done before it raised its left hand in a slow waving motion as if pleading. Genuine darkness descended all about them and far above, streaking across the sky was the darkest bat imaginable. They were aghast at its swiftness, mesmerized by its flapping wings as it darted across the horizon. They looked at one another in astonishment and then turned to look back at the dark figure. It was gone. It was then that Clara said, "Are we hallucinating? We did see an old man, a bat and a dark figure, right?"

Sue's father replied to his wife, "We did, yes, and that despicable man was scarcely human at all. It had the hideous face of some warlock, of some devil, something not of this earth. Yet, it must be, because it was a living, breathing thing. I have seen him before, seen that shadowy figure, too. Wait, wait – you know the paintings we bought from the antique store but never hung? We just put them away in the basement. I think they are representative of what we just saw. Come, this is a most curious situation indeed, and we will examine that painting."

Dina went on telling a story that captivated Sue and Lynton, relating that as the two walked back home, Clara related how she had seen that figure before outside the house, and how she had seen the bat at almost the same time. They got back home and immediately went downstairs to dig among the dusty and mouldy things that had been discarded long ago, until they found a frightening painting that they had once ignored but could no longer discount its relevance in regards to what they had just experienced. They looked at it in amazement. It was not very well done, but there in a forest, approaching out of a mist was an old man with gnarled face and right beside him was a pleasant looking little girl, but with evil eyes. They were both moving toward a dark figure that seemed to be motioning for them to stop, and high above all three was a bat streaking across the sky in front of a full moon. It was then that Clara turned to her husband Robert and said, "Let's take it upstairs and study it closer."

Dina had Lynton and Sue enthralled as she told how they studied it in the privacy of their bedroom until exhausted trying to figure out its meaning. It was then that Robert noticed something strange.

There was blood on his shirt over the right shoulder. He reached up and felt his neck on the right side and looked at Clara holding out his hand which was bloody. He pointed at her left chest and there was an obvious blood stain there. She felt her neck and brought down her bloody hand. She just stood there staring at it, totally baffled.

The extraordinary weight of the picture had struck both as very odd. They lifted it, and were bewildered about what made it so heavy. They shook their heads, put it out in the hallway and decided to have dinner as dark rain clouds gathered outside. The heat and oppression of the air increased and the night was exceedingly dark, and no twinkle of star or moon ray could penetrate the pall of cloud that overset the sky. Both of them had avoided discussing the blood on their clothing and the pain in their necks. However, as they took a seat on the veranda to observe the coming storm, something else occurred that precluded any discussion of the blood on their clothes. A bright oblong streak of light shone across the lawn to the iron gate which led on to the rough grass, where an ancient walnut tree stood. A wild dog stood outside the gate. It had all his hackles up, bristling with rage and fright; his lips were curled back from his teeth, as if he was ready to spring at something, and he was growling furiously. He took not the slightest notice of either person on the veranda, but stiffly and tensely walked across the grass to the iron gate. There he stood for a moment, looking through the bars and still growling. Then, all of a sudden, his courage seemed to desert him. He gave one long howl, and scuttled away with a curious crouching sort of movement. It was obvious that in that old walnut tree he had seen something that he hated and feared. Robert and Clara walked to the gate. Then they meandered toward the tree and looked over it from top to bottom. They saw nothing there at first. The rain began and they scurried inside, turned and looked back at that tree, where in a high branch was perched a huge bat.

Exhausted by a trying day, they went to bed and immediately drifted off to sleep. Clara's awakening occurred in a few hours, and she sat upright in bed under the impression that some bright light had been flashed in her face, though it was now absolutely pitch dark. She reached over to touch Robert, but he was not there. Suddenly, fear invaded and froze her brain. Immediately after a peal of thunder crackled just above the house, offering the probability that it was only a flash of lightning which awoke her gave no reassurance to her galloping heart. Something she knew was in the room with her, and instinctively she put out her right hand, which was nearest the side of the bed, to keep it away. And her hand touched the edge of a picture-frame propped up against the nightstand. She sprang out of bed, upsetting the small nightstand, and heard numerous items that had been on the nightstand fall to the floor. For the moment there was no need of light, for a blinding flash leaped out of the

J. Wayne Frye

clouds, and there propped up against the bed now was the painting. And instantly the room went into blackness again. But in that flash she saw another thing also, namely a figure that leaned over the end of her bed, watching. It was dressed as the little girl in the picture was, in some close-clinging white garment, spotted and stained with blood, and the face was that of the little girl in the portrait. Overhead the thunder cracked and roared, and when it ceased and the deathly stillness receded, she heard the rustle of movement coming nearer her and, more horrible yet, perceived an odour of corruption and decay. And then a hand was laid on the side of her neck, and close beside her ear she heard quick-taken, eager breathing. Yet, she knew that this thing, though it could be perceived by touch, by smell, by eye and by ear, was still not of this earth, but something that had passed out of the body and had power to make itself manifest. Then she thought to herself: "Why did I come to this forest to live? Something has been waiting for me here, waiting to feast on me, waiting in the mist and darkness to devour my very soul."

Why she had not screamed she did not know. Maybe the fear was just so intense she could not find her voice. She tried to scream desperately, but her voice would not follow her brain's command as the quick breathing came closer to her, so close that she could feel it breathing on her neck. At that, the terror, which had paralyzed her for the moment, gave way to the wild instinct of self-preservation. She hit wildly with both arms, kicking out at the same moment, and heard a little animal-like squeal and something soft dropped with a thud beside her. She took a couple of steps forward, nearly tripping over whatever it was that lay there, and by the merest good-luck found the handle of the bedroom door. In another second she ran out on the landing and had banged the door behind her as she heard the flapping of wings. Almost at the same moment she heard a door open somewhere below and saw Robert, who came running upstairs when he heard the noise.

"What is it?" he said. "Good heavens, there's blood on your shoulder."

She stood there in shock, and finally finding her voice, asked where he had been. He told her that he had been in the kitchen eating. She threw her arms around him, shivering in fear, swaying from side to side white as a sheet with blood on her left shoulder.

"It's in there," she said, pointing. "She, you know. The portrait is in there, too, leaning against the bed. That little girl. That girl, that little girl is in there I tell you."

Robert replied, "Darling, this is but a mere nightmare," as he quickly pushed by her and opened the door while Clara was standing there simply inert with terror, unable to stop him, unable to move.

"Phew! What an awful smell," he said.

Then there was silence, as he passed out of her sight, only to, in a few seconds, come out just as white as she was, instantly shutting the door behind him.

"Yes, the portrait's there," he said, "and on the floor is a small patch of dark earth, as if someone had feet that had walked on lose dirt. Come away, quick, come away."

How Clara got downstairs she hardly knew. An awful shuddering and nausea of the spirit rather than of the flesh had seized her and nearly seized Robert as well. She stood there clasping to Robert, while every now and then she cast glances of terror and apprehension up the stairs.

Dina took a deep breath and said, "That is what happened exactly as she shared it with me. They never again slept in that room. Rather, they had it and that picture up there sealed, ordering no servant to enter the room either, even to clean it. Eventually, as you know, they had the room sealed off with brick and mortar. It has been sealed all these years, and, for one, I have no desire to ever unseal it and cross that threshold. After that night and the eventual sealing of the room, the evil seemed to be held at bay, until the day your father was killed, Sue. Then it appears the forces of evil were unleashed again to wreck havoc on your father and mother. Maybe you cannot seal something that malevolent up. Perhaps it is only wishful thinking that it has been held at bay."

Lynton interjected, "And she said that the thing or whatever it was, she felt it had been waiting for her?"

"Yes, definitely."

Sue, looking forlornly at Lynton, said, "You are a world famous demon hunter, a woman who has dealt with these type things many times. I remember your encounter with the vampire, Ambrogio, as detailed in Wayne's books. Is this a similar occurrence?"

"Saying something now would only be conjecture, but I have an idea that whatever was seen that night has never been walled up. It was wishful thinking to believe you could destroy the evil so easily, and it is that evil which killed both your mom and dad. I also believe it has killed others, many others here in Ladysmith for many, many years."

Angus, quiet through it all, said, "Don't forget what Clara said after Robert's death. 'It has killed him.' That thing, whatever it is, is still at large, roaming Ladysmith, still contemplating evil in that infernal misty forest. There is evil all about."

Chapter 6
To Drink, To Drink

From the grave to wander, it is forced
To seek life's long severed link.
It craves for something that is lost,
And its lifeblood is to drink, to drink!

My dear young maiden clingeth
Unbending, fast and firm
To all the long-held teaching
That had people flinching
About vampires she thought true.
As in vampires immortal,
Folks thought they flew in a dark portal.
Most do it is a fact,
But in Ladysmith resides one causing fright,

Lynton and the Ladysmith Phantom

For it will appear in bright daylight.

It is the dreaded Dhampyr.
A vampire's vampire is it.
Oh, what a frightful sight
In bright daylight or darkest night.
As softly thou art sleeping,
To thee shall it come creeping,
And thy life's blood drain away.
And so shalt thou be trembling,
For thus shall it the neck be kissing,
And death's threshold thou be crossing.

From the grave to wander it is forced,
To seek life's long severed link.
It craves for something that is lost,
And its lifeblood is to drink, to drink!

"Lynton, are you saying there is among us here in Ladysmith a vampire?" asked Sue as they were joined by the Manly's.

"I am saying that I have encountered happenings similar to this in both the Philippines and in the mighty South African Karoo area."

Perplexed, Angus said, "This is preposterous. Vampires come out only at night according to legend. These sightings of hooded figures and bats have occurred in daylight as well as at night."

Lynton, letting a smile crease her lips, said, "Well, if you want real blood suckers, the very worst you can find are in banks or in the corporate boardrooms during the day, where the very life is sucked out of desperate people. The vampires of capitalism are the most insidious."

All there enjoyed the bit of levity that relieved the tension, but Lynton continued, "The idea of a vampire as a creature of the night is primarily a Hollywood creation, and like so many things Hollywood there is little correlation to truth. In Balkans folklore, Dhampyrs are creatures that are the result of a union between a vampire and a human. This union was usually between male vampires and female humans, with stories of female vampires mating with male humans being rare. These offspring between vampires and humans carry the power of the world's sun in their veins. That sunlight and eternal life offers unparalleled power. When normal vampires are exposed to direct sunlight they usually suffer great pain and diminishment of power, turn to dust or go up in flames but not so for Dhampyrs, as they can function in both day and night, and the strange thing is these creatures are unaware they are vampires until they reach a certain age, then the need for fresh human blood becomes overpowering. These are vampires that need human blood only 3 or 4 times a year, sometimes much less. They can even lead normal lives. What makes them so frightening is the fact they can freely walk around in sunlight. Either nothing at all happens, or they experience mild discomfort. Usually they are stronger during the night, with daylight taking away some of their powers, but otherwise they are fine. This was, in fact, the standard in traditional vampire lore and early vampire fiction long before Hollywood."

Though all there were skeptical, they did exhibit rapt attention as Lynton went on. "Fictional vampires, before Hollywood came on the scene, like Lord Ruthven, Varney the Vampire, Carmilla, Dracula and, of course, Ambrogio, could all prance around in broad daylight, and while some of these might be accustomed to sleeping during the day, daylight in itself was no danger to them. It was Hollywood that gave us the vampire that could only come out at night. Even the traditional vampire that comes out at night will not immediately be killed by the sunlight. It takes three or four hours of exposure, before they will succumb. Furthermore, although some vampires prefer to sleep in coffins during the day, it is not necessary. Nor is it necessary to have some earth from where they were buried."

"What of a stake thought the heart?" asked Sue.

"It works, but it must be precisely placed to penetrate the heart, which is actually not on the left side of the chest, but rather more centralized. The stake does not have to be made of wood. The truly most effective method is to decapitate the vampire and bury the head and body separately. Now, I know you all think this silly, but sometimes the silly has a grain of truth in it. I am not saying that vampires exist, but I am absolutely saying that evil exists; and thereby, it is advisable to have an open mind. An open mind means you are prepared for any eventuality in a world where evil is the ruling norm. There are good people in the world, but unfortunately there are far too few of them."

"How can one identify a vampire or a Dhampyr," asked Derek?

Lynton, familiar with vampire lore as a result of two encounters with Ambrogio as detailed in *Lynton and the Vampire at Tagatay Manor* and *Lynton, the Karoo Vampire and the Jewells of Omar Bin Abi*, willingly shared most of what she knew. "While most people can name several elements of vampire lore, there are no firmly established characteristics. Some vampires are able to turn into bats or wolves; others can't. Some are said not to cast a reflection, but others do. Holy water and sunlight are said to repel or kill some vampires, but not others. The one universal characteristic is the draining of a vital bodily fluid, typically blood, although the Philippines Aswang vampires prefer to dine on the blood of pregnant women only, while most vampires will partake of any available blood, even that of animals. One of the reasons that vampires make such successful literary figures is that they have a rich and varied history and folklore. Writers can play with the rules while adding, subtracting or changing them to fit whatever story they have in mind."

With a broad smile, indicating his complete scepticism for what appeared absurdities to him, Derek Manly said, "And just how do you know a vampire when you see one? Can you only tell when its teeth are on your neck?"

Lynton and the Ladysmith Phantom

Lynton sighed and looked a bit perturbed as she shook her head. "I know Derek that it considered nonsense in this day and age. I had the same reaction until I ran across Ambrogio twice in my adventures. Even now I am not sure if he is truly a vampire, but his obviously evil intentions when I encountered him are undeniable. Identifying a vampire is not always easy. According to one Romanian legend, you'll need a 7-year-old boy and a white horse. The boy should be dressed in white, placed upon the horse, and the pair set loose in a graveyard at midday. Watch the horse wander around, and whichever grave is nearest the horse when it finally stops is a vampire's grave or crypt or it might just be something edible nearby; take your pick. Interest and belief in revenants, meaning people who have returned from the dead, surged in the Middle Ages in Europe, although in most modern stories the classic way to become a vampire is to be bitten several times by one. Potential revenants can not generally be identified until after a certain age. The Dhampyr is almost impossible to identify, even after it comes of age. Of course, when a child is born as a result of a union between a vampire and a human there is sometimes a distinctive red mark under the hair on the right side of the head, a very small mark that appears to be in the shape of a bat's right wing. This is a definite indication that it must feed on the living. Many times if there were suspicions a woman copulated with a vampire, baby's heads were very closely

J. Wayne Frye

examined in places like Romania and many of the Caucus nations. If that sign was there, the baby would be beheaded and the two body parts placed in separate graves.

Shaking his head vehemently, Derek said, "And you expect us to believe there might be vampires among us here in Ladysmith? That the dark figure that Sue and I have seen – that you have seen – are actually vampires? People are embalmed today. They have no blood left in them. I want to believe, but I am just mystified by all this."

Very resolute in her demeanour, Lynton replied, "You need blood to exist if you are a vampire or Dhampyr, and they get that from an outside source. The belief in vampires stems from superstition and mistaken assumptions about post-mortem decay. The first recorded accounts of vampires follow a consistent pattern: some unexplained misfortune would befall a person, family or town like a drought drying up crops or an infectious disease. Before science could explain weather patterns and germ theory, any bad event for which there was not an obvious cause might be blamed on a vampire. Vampires were one easy answer to the age-old question of why bad things happen to good people. Villagers ignorantly combined their belief that something had cursed them with fear of the dead, and concluded that perhaps the recently deceased might be responsible, having come back from the grave with evil intent. Graves were unearthed, and surprised villagers often mistook ordinary decomposition processes for supernatural phenomenon. For example, though laypeople might assume that a body would decompose immediately, if the coffin is well sealed and buried in winter, putrefaction might be delayed by weeks or months or years; intestinal decomposition creates bloating which can force blood up into the mouth, making it look like a dead body has recently sucked blood. These processes are well understood by modern doctors and morticians, but in medieval Europe, before embalming, they were taken as unmistakable signs that vampires were real and unmistakingly existed. Now, we are all well-educated, well read and think we are too sophisticated to accept what we would assume is nonsense. I have lived in Africa, travelled Southeast Asia and seen, even heard things, that defy modern explanation. I am a realist, but I know there are things out there that simply defy explanation, even in the modern world."

Lynton walked over to the window, looked out at the mist forming below and said, "I am only relating to you what I have observed and read. The best way to deal with vampires, of course, is to prevent them from coming back in the first place. A few centuries ago in Europe this was often accomplished by staking suspected vampires in their graves; the idea was to physically pin the vampire to the earth, and the chest was chosen because it's the trunk of the body. This tradition was later reflected in popular fiction depicting wooden stakes though hearts as dispatching vampires. There was no significance to using wood according to folklore. Vampires, like genies and many other magical creatures, fear iron, so an iron bar would be even more effective than a wooden stake. Yet, again because of Hollywood, we have been conditioned to think only a wooden stake will do. Other traditional methods of killing vampires include decapitation and stuffing the severed head's mouth with garlic or a brick. In fact, suspected vampire graves have been found with just such signs. In 2013, archaeologists in Bulgaria found two skeletons with iron rods through their chests. It was postulated that the pair were believed to have been accused vampires."

"So, the methods of destroying vampires vary. In some traditions, the best way to stop a vampire is to carry a small bag of salt with you. If you are being chased, you need only to spill the salt on the ground behind you, at which point the vampire is obligated to stop and count each and every grain before continuing the pursuit. If you don't have salt handy, some say that any small granules will do, including birdseed or sand. Salt was often placed above and around doorways for the same reason, ditto with garlic. Some traditions hold that vampires cannot enter a home unless formally invited in. This may have been an early form of the modern *be leery of strangers* warnings to children, a scary reminder against inviting unknown people into the house. There are, of course, a few truly vampire animals, including leeches and bats. In most cases, the human-like vampire's intent is to draw just enough blood for sustenance, but not enough to actually kill the host. However, there are vampires that relish doing harm to victims and delightfully revel in the pure, systemic evil of what they are doing. There are also deranged people who invoke sick rituals that mimic vampire abominations, and that is what I hope we are dealing with here, deranged individuals. But alas, I can find no indication that there is not a supernatural element involved, an element that simply seems to defy explanation."

"Are there instances similar to what we are experiencing where vampires wrecked havoc on one town, one family, on one person," asked Sue.

"I have found out something my husband has hidden for a long time. I talked with him today, and related all that has occurred here. He steered me to his library, where he said I would find a poem anthology there by an obscure writer named Warren Harmon, and it contained a poem Wayne wrote when he first moved here way back in 2003, a poem that explained an odd occurrence he had heard about many years ago. He had kept me in the dark, because he feared my natural curiosity would get the best of me, but he now fears for your safety, Sue. He was told by someone about a Dhampyr right here in these woods that had such a frightening effect he wrote that poem about it," offered Lynton as she pulled a little book from her back pocket and began to recite:

There once descended a youth from the mountains

Lynton and the Ladysmith Phantom

Unto sleepy little Ladysmith town;
Eager to meet his new family, friends
And bride in waiting of great renown.
They had recently
Both been dearly paired,
Soon by wedding to be bound.

But will this warm and graceful welcome last,
If one so dearly has to pay?
He is still among a heathen class,
While she supposedly walks the Christian way.
With a new creed born,
With love and truth torn,
The dark night quickly consumes each day.

The castle already silently sleeps,
But something dead wakes.
Wishing him goodnight, the mother retreats.
Alone in his room now sleep waits:
Food and wine are laid,
And very lavishly displayed,
But he retires behind his silken drapes.

He cared neither for hunger nor for thirst.
He had no thought of senses' pleasures.
All were forgotten by his weary body.
Into bed he fell still sporting trousers.
And as he was almost slumbering,
A guest comes creeping
By his door, entering his sleeping quarters.

By his shimmering night lamp, he beholds

J. Wayne Frye   129

Lynton and the Ladysmith Phantom

A maiden wearing her veil and robe,
Appearing with angel's graces and silken folds,
And sporting a band of black and gold.
But as she sees him
By a light so dim;
She unveils a pallid hand very cold.

"Am I so forgotten in this household
That no word of a guest was sent to me?
Oh! How they in this prison chamber hold
Me, and in this deep shame keep me.
These dreams must now cease.
I must leave in peace,
And fade before anyone can see."

"Wait! Beautiful maiden," the young boy pleads,
Rising from his bed so quickly.
"Let us enjoy the gifts before us that seeds,
And welcome blushing cupid warmly.
Why now look so pale?
Why not sweetly hail
These gifts offered so graciously?"

"Stay away oh young soul! Stay far away.
Joy's grape no longer greets my pallet.
I know no bliss as dark consumes each day,
For my mother with her devout fears
Has taken her oath
And pledged my troth
To the grave with all my youthful years."

"The ancient throng of gods have taken flight.

Lynton and the Ladysmith Phantom

Our home has been emptied of their lore,
For unseen there lies in the heavens' light
A son who once mercifully bore
Man's every sin
To save our kin.
So we pledge our woe forevermore."

He listens, weighing every word she speaks,
Not one escaping his mind:
"I cannot fathom in such a quiet place
A dream I could have never feigned.
Oh but be mine now!
To you my love I will vow.
Our union has been ordained."

"My hand you cannot have faithful soul,
For my fair sister will be your delight.
Yet, when I am weeping in my dark cell,
Think of me as you hold her at night.
I think but of you.
I dream but of you,
Soon to hide my face where there is no light."

"No wait! By the sacred flame I already swore
That you would be kept on my love throne,
But let us not leave all forsaken.
Come with me to my home.
What should we fear
When there is so much cheer,
And a wonderful feast before us shown!"

Tokens of their faith were swiftly exchanged.

Lynton and the Ladysmith Phantom

She hands him a glittering chain of gold,
And he offers her an exquisite chalice
Of shining silver and beauty untold:
"This I cannot take,
But please for my sake,
Give me just one lock of your dark hair."

The unhallowed midnight hour bell rang.
Suddenly the maiden came alive.
With a parching thirst, she quickly drank
The dark blood coloured wine.
But of the wheat bread,
Upon which he fed,
She refused to take the slightest bite.

She handed her same cup to the youth,
And he, like she, quickly drank each drop.
He implored the maid for the truth.
Alas! Love had been lit in his heart.
But as he persists
She only resists,
Until weeping he sinks into bed.

The maiden pitifully leans over him
"Oh! How it pains me to see you so,
But were you to feel these limbs
You would shudder, knowing what they conceal.
A snow-white maiden
Whose blood is frozen,
Such is the love that these limbs reveal."

The ardent youth wraps his arms around her

Lynton and the Ladysmith Phantom

With the strength young love inspires:
"Were you risen directly from your grave
My love would set your every limb on fire."
Kissing and caressing,
Love shared was overflowing.
Between them was a burning desire.

Holding each other closely, neither contain
Their tears falling with the sweetest ardour.
His hot breath surges through her frame.
Each thinks of nothing but the other.
So a fiery flood
Warms her frozen blood.
But alas! No heart beats in her breast.

Meanwhile the devout mother makes her way
Through the halls. As she tends to her chores,
She hears a murmur and wonders what might lay
On the other side of one of those doors:
Wailing and crying,
Sobbing and sighing,
Who can allay love's frenzied pangs?

She halts in front of the door listening,
Hoping to convince herself that what she heard
Was nothing real. Then she hears lamenting
Entreaties and passionate parting words:
"Quick! The cock now crows,
But come tomorrow.
Won't you return for kiss on kiss."

Without hesitation, the mother quickly opens

Lynton and the Ladysmith Phantom

The door, anger swelling across her face:
"Such shameless scandals and unbridled sin
Made a home in my own hearth?" she screams
Looking through the door
At a sight to abhor,
Her dead daughter in the young man's embrace.

Terrified, the youth seeks to cover her,
Draping a white sheet over her head,
Yet she slyly slips from her lover's
Embraces, and she reveals herself:
With ghostly mien,
She begins rising
Like a wraith from the depths of the tomb.

"Mother! Mother! Give me one good reason why
I was born for loveless nights alone,
Ripped from love's warm embraces,
And left here only to pitifully moan.
You bereft my heart
Of both life and art,
And left it cold and sullen like a headstone."

"Alas in this frigid and dark cave,
I will end my wretched sleeplessness.
Your priests and their holy hymns can't save
Me, nor holy prayers from above.
Salt and water cools,
But my heart knows not fools.
The frigid grave cannot cool love!"

"My vows had already been pledged to this boy,

J. Wayne Frye

Lynton and the Ladysmith Phantom

When the world newly stood.
Mother, have you chosen to destroy
Sacred vows that you once understood?
No God lends his ear
To mothers who dare
Forsake one of their own innocent brood."

"Driven nightly from my grave, forsaken,
I walk this land in hopes of quenching
My desire for the one who'd been given
My hand to draw the blood from his being.
His life is now mine,
But there's one more to find,
As many helpless souls are still in waiting."

"Oh beautiful boy, your heart has run its course.
The dark forest below will soon be your grave.
While my love chain is wrapped around your neck,
This lock of your hair I'll gladly save.
Though now it is dark,
Soon it will be grey,
As its sable lustre flees the grave."

"Dear mother, this life has taken its toll:
Lay out a funeral pyre on this ground,
And let me grant succour to my wretched soul,
Finding the peace I've always longed for!
When glistening flames flow,
When the ashes glow,
Back to my youth I will soar."

"I have bitten my lover here,

And he shall bring his child into the world
Through my sister so dear.
Alas, he will plant his seed in her,
And in the heat of passion sworn
A Dhampyr shall be born.
This I swear shall occur."

"What exactly are you saying Lynton? Do you mean that a Dhampyr has inhibited this domain for all these years," asked Sue.

"I am saying that my husband told me the history that has apparently been hidden all these years. He put it all into a poem that he had gathered from various sources. The young man had been infected by the Dhampyr that coupled with him, and during the coupling she feasted on his neck just enough to turn him into a Dhampyr. He, in turn, over his mother-in-law's objections, coupled with his bride, and the result was a Dhampyr. That bat we have seen is a vampire. I am assuming that the dark hooded figure is the vampire's henchman. And that little girl you played with I assume was a ghost, but what her relationship is to the vampire I have no idea."

From the grave to wander it is forced,
To seek life's long severed link.
It craves for something that is lost,
And its lifeblood is to drink, to drink!

Chapter 7
She Died in 1957

On a mountainside a vampire is sent.
The corpse shall from its tomb be rent.
Then it will ghostly haunt its native place,
And suck the warm blood of the human race.

There from children, husbands and wives
It drains the stream of lives,
Yet loathes the banquet which perforce
Must feed its lonely living corpse.

Its victims ere, and then expire,
Knowing this demon for their sire,
Cursing it, while it curses them,
And flowers are withered on the stem.

It has been noted that without libraries there is no past and no future. It was Albert Einstein who said, "The only thing you have to absolutely know is where the library is located." However, the appearances of television and the internet diminished the intrinsic importance of libraries, unfortunately. Perhaps the masses embracing buffoons like Donald Trump is a direct result of the diminishing importance of libraries. When television becomes the source of all information, and organizations like FOX News spread fascist propaganda, the collective brains of the populace are turned into pliable mush, and independent thinking becomes a lost art. When people are more interested in what the Kardashians are doing, more enthralled with the latest appearances of prancing celebrity peacocks on Dancing with the Stars or sit on their sofas extolling the great contributions to society of basic illiterates who are paid millions because they can throw a great touchdown pass or hit a game-winning basket from midcourt, the hope for the future is dismal indeed. Fortunately, Lynton was one of those who did know the value of a library. For her, those stacks of books were portals that led her out of poverty, opened the doors of opportunity and brought sunshine to darkness. They were the stage upon which words opened the mind of hope. She understood that educated people were dangerous to the power structure, because they have a tendency to ask questions. Knowledgeable people bring shivers to those who are in control.

Lynton and the Ladysmith Phantom

Upon entering the small Ladysmith library, Lynton walked over to the stacks, and as she always does in any bookshop or library, looked in the fiction section to see how many of her husband's books were there. Of his 48 works, she disappointedly found but seven. Of course, she had higher respect for his talent than did most others. Was she prejudiced? Of course she was!

Was it by chance that Louise Appleby, a librarian, walked up and whispered over her shoulder, "I know you. I have seen your pictures in Wayne Frye's books. You are the demon hunter, Lynton Viñas."

Turning toward her, Lynton said, "I am, yes."

Louise, introducing herself, asked if there was anything she could help her find.

"Well, to tell the truth, I am looking for information on Dhampyrs. Do you know what they are?"

The woman, looking to be in her 80's, replied, "I am one of the few who would know around here. Of course, I am an old woman who has accumulated a lot of information from many sources here in the library. Many books have been tossed out over the years, but there were none I probably did not read, and I retain much of the knowledge. You will find no volumes here on Dhampyrs," and as she pointed toward a table in the far corner, she continued, "but if you desire to pick my ageing brain let's have a seat, and I will answer any questions you might have, within the limits of my knowledge, of course."

Lynton noticed other library patrons nearby looking at her strangely. She ignored their stares and took a seat next to Louise. She said to her, "Do you know of any strange occurrences hereabouts from years long past, occurrences involving the highly unusual that might be connected to disappearances in town, or strange manifestations of dark forces that might have come into play, forces of the supernatural?"

Still noting other patrons looking her way strangely, Lynton ignored them and anxiously awaited a reply.

Louise, her eyes twinkling with delight that someone was conversing with her, replied in a muted tone. "It is a sad story my dear, but let me share with you what I read of a strange occurrence from long ago, so strange that the manuscript recounting it was deemed too lurid, too petrifying to be maintained in the library. The censors of the area, at the time, preferred to control what the people could read, because they thought too much knowledge was a bad thing. Oh, and knowledge of any resident evil they feared might cause undue alarm. You see, those in power are fearful of people gaining too much knowledge, as I am sure you are aware, because people who think might demand answers to their questions."

"Yes, I agree with you Louise. Mass ignorance is actively promoted by those in power. Why do you think FOX News is so successful? It is easy to convince people to actually accept lies as truth when you capture their minds."

Lynton and the Ladysmith Phantom

When Louise said, "I have no knowledge of FOX News," Lynton was surprised, but then again FOX News had failed so miserably in Canada, because Canadians were more astute consumers of news than were Americans and understood the difference between genuinely real news and mere propaganda.

"What story can you share?" asked Lynton as she noticed how a few others in the library still seemed to be watching her intently. And what follows is the story exactly as it was shared by Louise.

It happened in the midst of the dissipations attendant upon an unusually vicious winter on Vancouver Island. There appeared from the far side of the mountain, in what is now Ladysmith, a rather young man named Malcolm, who displayed an incredibly striking bearing. From where he came no one knew. Not just one feature made him so handsome, though his eyes came close. People often spoke of the colour of eyes, as if that were of intense importance, and his were beautiful in any shade. From them came an acuteness, an honesty, a gentleness but also a look that said he was not one who should be trifled with. Perhaps this was what was meant in long gone days by a gentleman, not one of weakness or trite politeness, but one of great spirit and noble ways. What he was and what was beautiful about him came from deep within; it made women want to feel how his lips moved in a kiss. They, no doubt, wanted to sense his hands following the curves of their bodies. You just knew as each year passed the lines on his face would deepen, but for him the ageing process would make him more handsome still, as if his soul would shine through his skin. He had tousled dark brown hair, which was thick and lustrous, but his eyes were his most mesmerising feature. They were deep dark brown, with an intensity that seemed to penetrate your soul, boring deep into your psyche. His face was strong and defined, his features moulded from granite. He had dark eye brows, which sloped downwards in a serious expression. His determined countenance drew into a hard line across his face. His perfect lips seemed always ready to utter profundity that would spellbind anyone within range of his melodic voice. His strong hands, slightly rough from working, held anyone he touched, male or female, in rapturous respect of his strength. When he smiled, it etched its way across his face with an intensity that made you aware that within him was a deeply guarded secret. He gazed upon the mirth around him as if he could not participate therein. Apparently, the light laughter from others that attracted his attention took one gaze from him to quell, and throw fear into those breasts where evil thoughts might seriously reign. Those who felt this sensation of awe could not explain from whence it arose. Some attributed it to the intensity of the eyes, which, fixing upon the object's face pierced through to the inward workings of the heart, and fell upon the brain with a leaden ray that heavily weighed upon the psyche of all in his presence.

J. Wayne Frye

His peculiarities did not keep him from being invited to every house in the sparsely populated area at the time. All near and far wished to see him, and those who had been accustomed to a variety of excitement were pleased at having someone in their presence capable of engaging their attention. In spite of the deadly hue of his face, which never gained a warmer tint, either from the blush of modesty or from the strong emotion of passion, though its form and outline were beautiful, the nubile female hunters after notoriety attempted to win his attentions, and gain, at least some marks of what they might term affection. Anna Dumbarton , who had married for position rather than love, threw herself in his way to attract his notice, though in total vain. When she stood before him, though his eyes were apparently fixed upon hers, still it seemed as if she was unperceived. She, who had never been ignored before, was baffled at his lack of interest, and she left the field for others eventually, giving up her hopes for having another clandestine lover in her considerable cadre of lovers. But though the beautiful adulteress could not influence even the guidance of his eyes, it was not that the female sex was indifferent to his interests. Yet, such was the apparent caution with which he spoke to the virtuous wives and innocent daughters, that few knew that he ever addressed himself to females in general. He had, however, the reputation of a winning tongue; and people were moved by his apparent hatred of vice. He was most often among those females who form the boast of their sex from their domestic virtues, rather than being among those who sully it by their vices.

However, there was one woman who eventually attracted his attention. Annabel Longworth was a woman of unknown quality, as she arrived by stagecoach and took up residence at the only hotel thereabouts in the nearby town of Cedar. It so happened that Malcolm was living under the same roof and observed her being so beautiful and delicate that she might have formed the model for a painter wishing to portray on canvass the promised hope of the faithful in paradise, save that her eyes spoke too much mind for any one to look for long into their blackness.

Malcolm began to attach himself more and more to Annabel, but she was not terribly conscious of his love. Still, she always seemed to part from him with reluctance. Malcolm began to lay out plans to build a castle like estate on the land on the side of a mountain he had procured from a crown grant. He left one day determined to proceed to that mountainside and begin measurements for his giant home. When some people heard of his plan, they urged him not to build there.

He would have none of it, as he had already made up his mind. Yet, these people described it as a playground of evil, where rumour had it there were nocturnal devils about that danced in the twilight of wickedness. He made light of their representations, and tried to laugh them out of the idea; but when he saw them shudder at his daring he was silent.

One day when he was about to depart, the innkeeper came to the side of his horse and earnestly begged of him to return before night allowed the power of those beings in the forest to be put into action. He was however so occupied in his plans that he did not perceive that daylight would soon end, and that in the horizon there was one of those specks which, at that time of the year, so rapidly gather into a tremendous mass and pour all their rage upon the area. He mounted his horse, determined to make up by speed for his delay, but it was too late. Twilight, in the winter months on Vancouver Island, is nonexistent as immediately the sun sets and night begins.

Before he had advanced far, the power of the storm was above, and the echoing thunder had scarcely an interval of rest as thick heavy rain forced its way through the canopying foliage, while the blue forked lightning seemed to fall and radiate at his feet. Suddenly his horse took fright and galloped with dreadful rapidity through the entangled forest. The animal at last through fatigue stopped, and he found by the glare of lightning that he was in the neighbourhood of a hovel that hardly lifted itself up from the masses of dead leaves and brushwood which surrounded it. Dismounting, he approached, hoping to find someone to guide him back to the town of Cedar, or at least trusting to obtain shelter from the pelting of the storm. As he approached, the thunders, for a moment silent, allowed him to hear the dreadful shrieks of a woman mingling with the stifled, exultant mockery of a laugh continuing in one almost unbroken sound. He was startled, but roused by the thunder which again rolled over his head, he, with a sudden effort, forced open the door of the hut. He found himself in utter darkness. The sound, however, guided him. He was apparently unperceived; for, though he called, still the sounds continued and no notice was taken of him. He found himself in contact with someone who was in a dark cloak. He immediately seized the cretin, and he felt himself grappled by one whose strength seemed superhuman. Determined to sell his life as dearly as he could, he struggled; but it was in vain. He was lifted from his feet by the thing and hurled with enormous force against the wall across the room, and his enemy threw himself upon him and kneeling upon his breast, placed boney strong hands upon his throat. His powerful assailant bent over and tried to bite him on the neck. A rumble of thunder reverberated as the lightning shone on a face that seemed to be deathly white. Suddenly, his attacker instantly rose, and leaving the prey, rushed out the door into the darkness. The storm was then still, but Malcolm was incapable of moving. He lay there gazing intently at the ceiling of the hut. Finally hearing whimpering over in the far corner of the room, he looked about and, to his surprise; there was the lovely Annabel lying on the floor sobbing uncontrollably.

Malcolm rushed to her side. There was no colour in her cheeks, not even on her lips. Upon her neck was a gapping bloody wound with the marks of teeth on an opened vein. He lifted her into his arms, found his horse outside, mounted it and rode furiously toward the doctor who lived in Cedar. Annabel was put to bed and was seized with a most violent fever and was often delirious. In these intervals she would call out the name Ambrogio, which her assailant had whispered.

Hearing the name of Ambrogio, with whom she had battled two times now, Lynton took a deep breath and sighed. Wayne was not going to like this. She had dealt with Ambrogio and lost in the battle to stay his evil in the Philippines, and then she dealt with him in South Africa, and again only marginally ended his reign of terror. She nodded her head in encouragement for Louise to continue her story, because she felt that she was beginning to get a handle on exactly what was going on with all the appearances of the shadowy figure and the ultimate disappearance of so many.

As Lynton said to her, "Go on with your story please," she noticed again that some patrons turned to stare at her with looks of bewilderment, as if she was perhaps a bit touched with some form of lunacy.

Louise described how the RCMP officer in Cedar thought that Malcolm was trying to shield his own attack on Annabel, but the innkeeper told him that it was highly unlikely that occurred, because he had seen Malcolm leave alone and had, in turn; seen Annabel about the hotel after Malcolm had left. Then, when Annabel regained the ability to speak she wove a tale that was so frightening that the RCMP officer told her that he could not report such a preposterous story, as his superiors would not believe him. Despite telling her it must have been a delusion caused by fear, she insisted it was not, and asked how she could have wound up at that hut in the forest on the side of the mountain in Ladysmith if it was a delusion.

According to her, she had gone to her room and decided to take a nap just as the sun disappeared behind the horizon. As she lay there in the twilight, an intense darkness suddenly descended upon the room. By the slightly open window, she saw a hand from the outside slowly raising it. Just as she started to scream, the window was pushed completely up, and then into the room bounded a menacing dark figure in what looked like a black cloak. The figure was so fast that before she could let out a scream it was upon her with a hand clasped over her mouth. That was the last thing she remembered except for a feeling of being in flight for awhile, until she woke up in that hut with a thing bending over her, sucking blood from her neck. She screamed furiously, but what good was it out in the wilderness away from where those screams could be heard by anyone? She then looked over at Malcolm and said that she vaguely remembered him lifting her up and holding her on his horse until they arrived at the doctor's, where she passed out.

J. Wayne Frye

Malcolm's mind, despite the shock of what he had experienced, was not swayed from starting his home on the side of the mountain, but he was now a lover of solitude except for Annabel, as they became inseparable. Her form stood by his side almost continuously, except an occasional sojourn into those misty woods. She would be gone for maybe thirty minutes, only to return in a somewhat ruminating state. He always observed continuously her pale face and wounded throat that seemed to not be healing, despite the doctor's assurance that it would over time.

Her step was light footed, as she strayed wherever a butterfly or a colour might attract her attention. She was sedate and pensive. When coming back from her walks into the forest her face was never brightened by the smile of joy, but when Malcolm started telling her of his growing affection she seemed to light up with great joy. Yet, it appeared that she was playing in the light of her own native sphere, a sphere where some dark secret was being guarded. Still, the two of them eventually became engaged, then married and continued to build the castle-like mansion that was now the home of Sue Fong. It consisted of four large rooms on the ground-floor, an entrance hall, a drawing-room, a sitting parlour, and a huge bedroom, along with servants' quarters. They were all simply decorated with plain dark-stained walls, marble tables on either side, a large rounded sofa in the centre of the foyer, and a small fountain near the entryway on the main floor. There were many statues all about, adding an air of sophistication. In the hall stood half a dozen cane chairs, and to one side was a large empty room except for bookcases, which contained no books in the beginning but eventually became the library that was lovingly stocked by Angus after the house passed into the hands of the Fong family. There were, at the insistence of Annabel, no mirrors, nor a single painting except for one that hung in the hallway. The painting was of a dark hooded figure in the forest with a young female child beside it, and above, flying across in front of a full moon was a giant bat. The bedrooms upstairs were somewhat stark except for one at the far end of the house which had a large balcony that looked out over the mist-covered forest in the distance. The appearance of the house externally was not pleasing but somewhat stark.

As mentioned previously, there was no town at the time, as the nearest one was Cedar, which was fifteen kilometres away, so there was an intense loneliness that seemed to permeate the estate. For years there was another huge estate on the other side of the mountain. It had been erected by a man named Blackie Redwood of whom very little was known. He had come from Europe, but he avoided contact with most people as Blackie brought his wife and two children with him. However, they lived in complete solitude and were rarely seen. There was an almost immediate dislike that developed between Blackie and Malcolm, but no one was sure why. The hatred simmered for years.

The marriage between Malcolm and Annabelle was somewhat sexless, as there was little physical affection from Annabel, but there was no doubting the love between them. One could sense a devotion to each other that was intense, so intense that the servants would often remark to one another that the two of them seemed, despite the often morose atmosphere of the household, truly happy when they were in each others presence.

There was a seat built onto the bedroom balcony upstairs, where Annabel would sit for hours looking into the forest, especially as the mist would slowly rise. Once or twice a month she would journey into that area alone, then return to her husband with a sullen demeanour. Still, Malcolm, although becoming more morose at what seemed to be his wife's oft indicated lack of zest for life, truly loved her and did all he could to bring her joy.

When Annabel announced that she was pregnant, she did so with what appeared to be deep remorse, actually apologizing to her husband. However, Malcolm embraced the news with great euphoria and had grand expectations for the arrival of an heir and son, but when Annabel had a daughter; he was just as excited and said, "A daughter is even better than a son, especially when she looks so much like you."

Once the child was born, Annabel seemed a less than devoted mother who was rather negligent. Then something happened that marked a dramatic turn, a turn that finally came to a head only one day after the child's third birthday when Annabel's husband saw her about to commit an unspeakable act. He walked into the nursery, and saw Annabel placing a pillow over the child's face. He rushed to the child's side, pulled the pillow off and pushed Annabel away, who dissolved into tears as she cried, "You do not understand! She is not your daughter. She is a spawn of hell."

"What do you mean?" asked Malcolm.

Annabel replied, "She is the daughter of evil, the daughter of a most despicable and vile creature. She was conceived in a union with wickedness, a union between woman and beast."

Malcolm looked over at the table where he gazed in shock at a large bone saw. He turned and asked Annabel what it was for. She replied, "For ending the evil that is growing each and every day, an evil that will eventually be unleashed to the detriment of both you and me, to the detriment of all anywhere near this abomination I have brought into the world."

From that day forward, Annabel and Malcolm grew distant, and she was never allowed to be alone with the child. Malcolm loved the child as he never had loved anything before. His devotion to her was unquestionable. Then, about three months after the incident, Annabel managed to slip into the child's bedroom, took it by the hand and led it down the mountainside into the misty forest below. What happened is unknown, but I share with you what was reported to the police.

After an exhaustive search, the child was found sitting on the ground in the forest leaning against a tree. At her feet was her dead mother. The mother had deep bite marks on her neck and all the blood had been drained from her body.

The child was questioned, but what could a three year old offer other than to say, "Mommy went to sleep."

Afterward, Malcolm's devotion to his daughter intensified, but she, like her mother before her, would often disappear into the misty forest to play, coming back with delightful smiles on her face. Within that forest dead animals that had the blood drained from them were often found. Malcolm, loving father that he was, doted on his daughter, but often reflected back on the time he had caught his wife trying to kill her. Why? Why? Why? He asked himself that question daily, and finally, after some research in nearby Victoria, he thought he had arrived at the answer, an answer that sent shivers through him. His daughter was a Dhampyr. His wife was right about the child not being his. He realized his wife's journeys into the forest were to mate with a vampire, and he knew who that vampire was.

Lynton looked at her with intensity as she asked, "What was the daughter's name?"

Louise Appleby replied, "Why her name was Lizzie."

Lynton said, "Of course – Elizabeth!" as again she looked at a few people staring at her as if she was crazy.

Lynton took her eyes off Louise for a second, looked out the window and saw Sue walking toward the front door. She said to Louise, "Be right back. It's my friend."

She met Sue at the front door and walked back toward where she and Louise were sitting. Louise was gone. Lynton walked over to a nearby table and asked a woman if she had seen where the lady she was talking to went. The reply was, "What lady? You were talking to yourself." She then realized why everyone had been staring at her.

She and Sue looked at each other in astonishment and proceeded to the check-out desk where Lynton asked the attendant if the librarian, Louise Appleby, was available. She replied, "Louise Appleby died in 1957."

Chapter 8
On My Killing Spree

One that for eternity must fall;
The little girl, best beloved of all,
Made her father shiver at mention of her name,
For it wrapped his heart in flame!

He knew he must end her task and mark,
Her cheek's last tinge - her eye's last spark
With the final glassy glance of a view
That must freeze o'er her body lifeless and blue.

Then with unhallowed hand he knew to tear
The tresses of her soft hair;
Of which, in life a lock when shorn
Affection's fondest pledge was worn.

Lynton and the Ladysmith Phantom

Borne away by death to be free
The father must endure agony!
With gnashing teeth and haggard lip,
He knows from her blood shall drip.

Then stalking to her sullen grave,
He goes where ghouls and vampires rave,
Till these in horror shrink away
From a spectre more accursed than they.

She is but a creation of evil
Sired to dance with the devil.
Like a cold winter growl,
She is a Dhampyr on the prowl.

Lynton shared with Sue all that she had learned from the phantom called Louise, and told her that she had deduced many things, but wanted to call Derek, Wilton, Angus and Dina together to share what she now thought was the key to the mystery. Before that though, she and Sue went to the RCMP office in town where she asked for access to records of disappearances in the area as far back as possible. Although there was reluctance on the clerk's part, the public was allowed free access to public records, and there was nothing that could prevent the two from poring over the now computerized materials, as long as there was not a current investigation. Fortunately, records went back over one hundred years, and it was remarkable how three or four people every year disappeared under unusual circumstances.

J. Wayne Frye

Lynton and the Ladysmith Phantom

Most of those who disappeared were First Nations, which meant little effort was expended to find them. This was the norm for those years before the 1970's, as just like the USA today, people of colour were marginalized and considered disposable. Canada was different, but there were still isolated areas where prejudice was inbred and promoted by those who always need someone to look down on, because the power structure wants people to blame the blameless rather than the real culprits of social and economic inequity – the privileged class. All you need do is look at the phenomena of the 2016 Presidential election in the USA to see how effective the privileged class is at shifting blame for economic inequities. Despite his fascism and blatant racism, Donald Trump remained popular among about 45% of the population and even though he lost the popular vote by three million, he became President because the USA is not a democracy as most Americans are propagandized into believing. That nation was originally set up by a pack of oligarchs who wanted to avoid paying taxes on their wealth to England, so they came up with a grandiose idea to convince common people how much they would gain by breaking away from England. The nation was founded by hypocritical bigots who had the unmitigated gall to actually put in the Constitution that all men are created equal while almost all of the signers of that Constitution were slaveholders. In America, the people who support bigoted, misogynistic, xenophobic, privileged narcissists like Donald Trump believe lies are better than facts, promises are better than accomplishments, comic books are better than Shakespeare, superstition is better than science and ignorance trumps intelligence. Lynton was a woman with deep rooted character who had trouble understanding how anyone with a moral core could be so easily manipulated that they would support a treasonous, totally corrupt, self-serving, racist, semi-literate, moronic, sexually assaulting, pathologically lying, feeble-minded, morally bankrupt, bloated nitwit with cotton-candy hair, radioactive spray-bottled tinted skinned obese prancing peacock as their leader. She felt that was the irony of modern America, where education is actually intentionally made unaffordable, because those in power do not want an educated populace that might actually challenge the authority of the entrenched, privileged oligarchy that fools the masses into believing anyone can make it in such a grand and equalitarian nation. Furthermore, the immense religious power structure is given even greater tax breaks than the wealthy to peddle an idea that promises pie in the sky in the sweet by and by where those denied the good life while alive will one day walk streets of gold in that magic kingdom up in the sky. Unfortunately, the rest of the world is only marginally better than the USA when it comes to coddling the rich and privileged. The world is a playground for the rich and a cesspool of lost hope for everyone else. This is

J. Wayne Frye

why the rich are like vampires according to Lynton. They prey upon the unsuspecting and despicably suck the very life out of the middle class and poor to satiate their own perverse desires for more and more. That was the way of a world where greed was promoted as an enviable trait, and an evil system called capitalism allowed those at the top to accumulate material wealth on the backs of the exploited poor and middle class. Lynton knew first hand the evil of that system, because the formally prosperous Philippines, where everyone once had shelter, a job and sustenance under a benevolent dictator, was handed over, at the insistence of the USA, to corporations and the wealthy to rape, plunder and pillage those at the bottom of the economic ladder.

She was furious about the fact that in all these years nothing had been done to bring justice to the families of those who had disappeared. They were mostly poor First Nations people who had their land stolen long ago by the white man, then became victims of white religious society that put them on reserves, in residential schools and destroyed their culture, a culture that believed no man could own the land, because it belonged to all, not just the few who wanted to fence it off and proclaim, "this is mine." These were people who could not understand greed, and how it was an obsession that permeated their oppressors' psyches to the point that owning more and more was the driving force that fuelled an economic machine which ground up people under the jackbooted tyranny of capitalism to bow before the mighty engine of brutal injustice and inequity.

Lynton was a woman with great desire and determination to root out the evil of those who preyed upon the unfortunate, whether it was economic, religious or sexual exploitation. She stood like the Rock of Gibraltar against the evils promulgated by the unfair distribution of wealth, and she was just as tenacious when it came to the real physical vampires as she was when it came to the clandestine vampires of commerce and politics.

As she assembled all at Sue's house, after explaining what she had learned, she said, "I am angry about what has been going on for over one hundred years. The authorities have turned a complete blind eye to evil. Why? Because that evil has been perpetrated all these years on the vulnerable in society: on the poor, on the forgotten and on people of colour. What I am about to say will not be pleasant, but it will explain what has happened here recently is the result of over a one hundred year reign of terror perpetrated by evil entities that know no boundaries in their obsessive search for victims to keep them alive forever."

"Let me tell you something that Sue and I discovered in the records of the local RCMP office." Then she removed from her carrying case a ream of printed papers copied from the records she and Sue reviewed in the Royal Canadian Mounted Police archives. "We discovered there a bevy of documents that should have been reviewed by appropriate authorities in regards to disappearances, but they did not care, because almost all who have disappeared around here have been First Nations and the poor. There was a man named Abraham Van Helsing, who was a famous vampire hunter, and he came to these shores in 1899 in search of someone I have encountered twice, the absolute most horrible phantom of mayhem, Ambrogio. This Van Helsing was assumed by the RCMP to have taken the name from Bram Stoker's Dracula novel. However, the truth is that there really was a man named Van Helsing from Amsterdam, and he had a reputation for being a vampire hunter. This person was the prototype for the character in Stoker's *Dracula* novel. Stoker described him as a man of medium height, strongly built, with his shoulders set back over a broad, deep chest and a thick neck. The poise of the head struck all as being indicative of thought and power. The head was noble, well-sized, broad and large behind the ears. The face was clean-shaven and showed a hard, square chin, a large resolutely mobile mouth, a good-sized nose that was rather straight, but with quick, sensitive nostrils that seemed to broaden as the upper lip came down and the mouth tightened. The forehead was broad and fine, rising at first almost straight and then sloping back above two bumps or ridges wide apart, such a forehead that the reddish hair could not possibly tumble over it, but fell naturally back and to the sides. Big, dark blue eyes were set widely apart."

Taking a deep breath, Lynton continued, "Now, I give you this description in detail, because the irony is that this description was almost verbatim the same description in the police report on Van Helsing's arrest for trespassing on someone's property here; the exact address being redacted. It is my opinion these two men were one and the same. Van Helsing was given a large fine and ordered out of Canada by a judge in Victoria, who found his story of a vampire in the Ladysmith area absolutely preposterous. He was tempted to have him sent to a mental institution for evaluation, but decided to simply order him out of Canada and let the Netherlands deal with him."

"Van Helsing was afraid to return to Vancouver Island, because of the fear he might be arrested again and put in a mental institution, but it is obvious to me that what he found was much more than Ambrogio. I believe he discovered a Dhampyr that was so frightening that he alerted the RCMP, but they simply dismissed him as a lunatic. He encountered this evil and tried to slay it by traditional methods, but was arrested with a wooden stake and a wooden hammer as he was about to break into the house where he maintained the vampire lived. He was held in a psychiatric ward in Victoria, but he was ordered to return to the Netherlands. As stated, the account we read was highly redacted, so there was no discernable description of the supposed vampire. However, I am beginning to form the nucleus of an idea."

"And what is that idea?" asked Derek.

Lynton and the Ladysmith Phantom

"Believe me; Van Helsing knew that he was after a vampire far more sinister than Dracula, because I have tangled with Ambrogio, myself. This is as devious a phantom as every flapped wings in the darkness of the night that wraps evil in its grasp like it is loved, adored and actually worshipped. What he has done here is as abominable an act as any he has ever committed, because he has sired an offspring that is almost as evil as he is. Angus, based upon your penchant for reading every book in this library, I am sure you are very familiar with Ambrogio, because I saw the two books in your stacks written by Wayne that featured him as a central character. This vampire of old arrived here by the commonplace means for the time. He sailed by ship to Victoria and took the train to Nanaimo and then a coach from there to here. You might think I am joking, or perhaps that by the word vampire I mean a financial vampire, as those types we must deal with every day. The only difference is that those vampires do not suck blood. They suck money. They suck your soul. They suck the life out of your heart. However, the vampire of whom I am speaking laid waste to family after family in his evil pursuit of that elixir of life that has sustained him for almost 500 years. Vampires are generally described as dark, sinister-looking and singularly evil. This vampire was normal in appearance, and at first sight was not sinister-looking, but rather seemed a bit nondescript. He went by the alias, Blackie Redwood, and I can assure you that most people he met came under his spell of fascination, as he was a smooth gentleman with an air of sophistication. He found a human named Annabel that he wanted to turn, and gradually he got her under his control. He lured Annabel, and made her into a virtual slave to his machinations. He then coupled with her, and the result was something Van Helsing found that was almost as sinister as Ambrogio, because the child named Elizabeth was born as a result, born to be a Dhampyr, and as a child, her victims were easy prey, because who could expect a mere child of such evil intentions?"

"After the death of his wife, people added to Malcolm's name the word *Dark* which was used to describe him because he became so morose at her loss that his only sign of happiness was his daughter, but soon even that happiness was shattered as a result of the activities of Blackie Redwood, who in reality was the vampire, Ambrogio. My guess is that as Elizabeth grew, Blackie began to regularly lure her into the forest, and Malcolm began to see her gradually change over the years, change into what could only be termed an evil entity that needed to feed occasionally on fresh animal blood, but he began to worry that eventually she would, like her abominable biological father, have to feed on human blood."

Dina, with what seemed trepidation, said, "It is known that Blackie kidnapped Elizabeth. Was that because he felt she was in danger from Dark Malcolm?"

"It was." replied Lynton. "In my opinion, Dark Malcolm came to the conclusion that in order to save Elizabeth and to assure that there would be no victims when she needed human blood every few months for sustenance, the only course for him was to kill her, and that is why he went to Blackie's estate. He did not go to return Elizabeth home, but to drive a stake through her heart and end her life for her sake and the sake of future victims here in Ladysmith. He knew that her real father was Blackie Redwood or as is now obvious, Ambrogio. His love for her meant that he had to end her agony, the agony of depending on fresh blood to survive."

"Are you saying," asked Dina, "that all these disappearances over the years are directly related to a Dhampyr, and that Dhampyr is the little girl Elizabeth who was the child of Ambrogio and Annabel?"

"Yes."

"But didn't Dark Malcolm slay her with a wooden stake through the heart?" asked a puzzled Dina.

"That is where we have a problem. I believe he thought he destroyed her. Remember how they were found embracing each other, as if father and daughter had been miraculously reunited, and then died in each others arms. The assumption was Dark Malcolm had gone there to do battle with Blackie Redwood and rescue Elizabeth who had been kidnapped, but I believe he went there solely to kill Elizabeth, to make sure she was freed from the tyranny of Ambrogio and the terrible fate of being a Dhampyr. The trouble is he assumed driving the stake though her heart would end the agony she was enduring. He drove it through her back, assuming it would penetrate her heart, but he failed to realize the heart was more centered in the chest, so he missed the heart, probably by a centremetre or less, and the wooden stake went through her chest into his. It was assumed she and her father were both dead, and they were buried here on the side of the mountain. We must find Elizabeth, and then end this terror the way Dark Malcolm should have ended it, by severing her head from her body and burying the remains in separate places."

Wilton Manly said, "And what of my dear wife? You think she was taken by this abominable creature, by this little girl who becomes a vampire of horrors?

"Unfortunately, yes I do. I think all these disappearances, or at least the vast majority of them are a result of these people being taken by a huge bat, a bat that is a shift-shaped Lizzie who is forced to live off the blood of animals until, like all Dhampyrs, she has the uncontrollable urge for fresh human blood. Now, I also have a theory about the dark, shadowy figure that seems to always appear prior to this bat sweeping down to snatch these people, snatch them and take them to what I believe is a killing ground in that forest. If we look hard enough, I believe we will find mass graves or a dumping ground in that forest."

Lynton and the Ladysmith Phantom

Wilton Manly was almost in tears as he arose and looked directly at Lynton. His voice quivered with emotion as he said, "You mean my wife is lying out there somewhere in some unmarked grave? You mean some evil thing has used her for blood and then discarded her, thrown her out like garbage?"

Derek got up and moved to his dad, wrapping him in his arms, as he said, "We will find her, dad. We will find mom's remains and we will also find this Dhampyr and destroy her, and along with her that despicable black shadowy figure that is a harbinger of coming evil."

Lynton, serious and direct, said, "We will find the bodies. I know they are out there. I know that Lizzie has a lair somewhere in that damnable forest, but I am not as sure about that dark figure being so sinister. I believe that it might well not be as malignant as one might think."

In the dark forest, as Lynton and the others plotted their sojourn into Lizzie's realm, there among the moss laden trees in a well concealed haven of evil was the one they sought, but her eternal childhood was, to her, more curse than a forever living blessing. She hated her existence, but what could she do? Lizzie, through no choice of her own, was a Dhampyr. She was contemplative, as she prepared to suck on the rabbit, its hairy white fur sticking to her lips as she prepared to devour with less than delight the elixir of life for her – fresh blood, but she felt the coming urge that was now becoming all consuming, an urge she had tried to suppress the few times a year that it overwhelmed her. She realized that her craving for human blood was now becoming more rampant than ever before.

Lizzie about to suck blood from a rabbit.

Lynton and the Ladysmith Phantom

She looked over at the dark shadow crouching in the corner of the cave, and realized that it was there out of love, a love that wanted to free her of the madness, but her lust for blood would have no patience for anything that stood between her and the sustenance she needed. She remembered being a little child, a limber elf, singing, dancing to herself, a fairy thing with red round cheeks that always wanted a playmate and finally found one long ago, found that little girl named Sue. However, she knew where that friendship would end, which was why she terminated it abruptly, but lately she found herself wondering how the friendly blood of the one she once played with might warm her cold body in a special way. Sue was an adult now, and her body had an abundance of warm, delicious, tangy red blood that would provide an elixir of euphoric delight. She had been making plans for weeks to swoop down from the night skies and snatch Sue, bring her back to her lair and deliciously and slowly dine on the special blood that would bring her the greatest delight ever experienced. She had tried to stymie her desire for Sue's blood by taking Harry Stammer from the motel, but her need for blood was not satiated anymore like it once was. She now needed human blood more often, and as she dined on the rabbit's blood she knew that the blood of animals no longer provided her with the exhilaration she craved. She hated what was happening, but what could she do? There was no way for her to curb the appetite for human blood anymore. Animals no longer satisfied her need for the one elixir that lifted her spirits and made her feel almost human. How she longed to be free of this curse!

She remembered how she once filled her human father's eyes with delight, but how that changed to sadness, when he realized what she was. The unsuccessful attempt to end her pain with death failed. That attempt had led to Ambrogio (Blackie Redwood) fleeing Ladysmith and finding new haunts to satisfy his quest for human blood. He had left his daughter behind, whispering in her ear to arise, as he removed the stake from her back, telling her to find a place to hide, because there around Ladysmith she was offered fertile hunting grounds to satisfy her need for human blood a few times a year. She pleaded with him not to leave her, but he explained that his wife and children could not accept a Dhampyr, because they were all vampires.

She was left by her human father's side, and so strong was his love for Lizzie that his dark spirit raised from his dead body to express love's excess, vowing to never leave her. Upon his heart were thoughts that he could not utter in speech any longer of the broken dream that he embraced with deep compassion. He was prepared to do her bidding now, to dally with harm for others to comfort the one he loved. He had tried to slay her for her sake to spare her the agony of a constant search for blood to satisfy the appetite for eternal life. Still, his compassion had sowed within him a desire to save the victims with warnings.

J. Wayne Frye

Lynton and the Ladysmith Phantom

Perhaps 'tis tender too and pretty
At each wild word to feel within
A sweet recoil of love and pity.
And what, if in a world of sin,
Such giddiness of heart and brain
Comes seldom save from rage and pain?

In the darkness of the cave they called home, this spirit of a man had not the capacity of speech and neither did his daughter, but they had love for one another, a love bonded and solemnized in a mutual understanding that they were both spirits bound inexplicitly to one another. Still, she was the superior spirit by nature of her being a Dhampyr, and he knew that her wish was his command, but that command to procure subjects for her vile need to drink the warm blood of the living nauseated him, made him long for the peaceful relief of a permanent grave where he and she might one day rest in peace and she would be free of this raging need for the blood of living creatures.

She, with a sinister grin, raised the rabbit to her mouth and bent over to bite the neck, so she could suck out the elixir that she so desperately needed. Her right hand gripped the back of the neck, and she forced her face down on the pulsating artery of the scared, shaking animal. Her white dress about to be smeared with blood in the same place it was always smeared, and a thin stream of blood trickled down her chin as the animal let go of life, going completely limp. Her eyes glassed over as she made gurgling sounds, lapping away like a hungry kitten before a warm bowl of milk.

They don't seem to notice me,
Just another little girl, so innocent.
Death comes in many a degree,
And I will hunt with abandonment,
As I go joyously on my killing-spree.

Chapter 9
The Night is Long That Never Finds the Day

The thin grey cloud is spread on high.
It covers delicately but does not hide the sky.
The full moon is dull; such an eerie sight,
As Lizzie now looks evil and about to bite.
The night is chilled, the cloud is grey,
And Lynton to the lair makes her way.

It was late, nearing midnight when Lynton, with her charges, set out in search of the lair. She knew that a Dhampyr could not resist the call of the full-moon at midnight. What must be done was to watch the bat soar upward toward the moon and then follow its trajectory downward. That would be the location of the lair.

Lynton and the Ladysmith Phantom

Trudging through the misty thick forest, owls were hooting, which was the only sound besides the crunching of leaves under their feet. Lynton stole along with the others. No words were spoken as all eyes kept glancing up toward the moon. There was a chill in the air, as was usual at night. They heard a long, whining moan, most likely a nearby creature that was offended by the human intrusion. Lynton signalled them to stop as she stood beneath a huge, broad-breasted, old arbutus tree. A slight breeze began to whisper the lonely sounds of night. The wind was not intense enough to twirl the lone leaf still on the tree that danced hanging so light and high on the topmost twig that looked up at the dull moonlit sky.

Their hearts were beating fast, as suddenly they saw a damsel-like bat soaring toward the moon. Half bat and half human, Lizzie's stately neck glistened under the moonlight, and her blue-veined feet flicked up and down, as if she was swimming. Wilton, the only religious one there whispered, "Mary mother save us now."

Sue said in a voice faint and with a tinge of fright, "I fear what is afoot. Surely, we are treading on evil ground here."

Chivalrously, Derek took her hand, squeezing it gently as he whispered so low no one else could hear, "I am by your side, and I vow to not take flight no matter how much I might be overcome with fright. You have endured the unendurable, and I pledge with all my heart undying devotion to you."

J. Wayne Frye

Lynton and the Ladysmith Phantom

Sue had been searching for love all her life, the kind of love that elevates the soul, the kind of love that flows through the body like a raging river through a gorge, the kind of love that dances in the bright light of hope, the kind of love that basks in the knowledge that life offers the possibility of fulfillment in the arms of a lover who elevates the soul and compounds the spirit. She had found it.

It was a lovely sight to see as the two stood by the old arbutus tree amid the jagged shadows of mossy leafless boughs. They kneeled in the moonlight, looking into each others eyes. It was as if they were sharing a dream of blissfulness. Derek did not hold her in his arms, but one could see his growing desire to do so. It was as if they were in the peaceful slumber of affection. The stillness of the night was a soft testament to the growing love, a love that they both desperately needed to bring fulfilment to two lives that had been thrown asunder for so long as they both had lost so much to the world of darkness that always seemed to blot out the sunshine of hope.

The scene made Lynton long for Wayne who was still on the dreaded book tour, while he was frantically trying to finish up his latest novel. On top of that, being separated made them both despondent for the warmth of one another's arms. Still, Lynton's heart was filled with joy that Derek and Sue had found one another, because love makes one completely human; makes one feel, give, take, laugh, get lost, be found, dance, love, lust and be wrapped in the warmth of affection.

Lynton and the Ladysmith Phantom

The ever sensitive Lynton looked at them as she longed for Wayne. Lovers, she thought, were like air bubbles on water, hastening to flow together. Constantly, as if looking through a remote skylight where the stars glistened and sparkled from a limitless heaven, she had glimpses of her serene love for Wayne, the conjunction of souls like waves which meet and break, but also subside backward over things, and thereby give all of life a fresh aspect. She had once given up hope, as had Wayne, but together they listened with one ear to each sound of life to behold with one eye the warm scene of affection, and they saw the visual rays of love meet and mingle to be mixed in harmonious union with the elixir of affection.

Despite the feeling of joy at the budding romance, Lynton knew there was no time to lose. From her trusty vampire fighting bag that she had used before in encounters with Ambrogio and his minions, she pulled a modern version of a plotting sextant and aimed it toward the bat in the sky. A trajectory line flashed across the screen and she got the exact coordinates of where the bat had come from far below. She said, "Hurry, we must prepare for Lizzie's return, prepare to end this reign of terror."

Gradually the realization overwhelmed these six intrepidly determined denizens of righteous indignation that they were about to embark on the fiery current necessary to end the nightmare of evil, while they floated in their raging minds from past to future as they silently embraced their destiny. They did not wish to kill or to be killed, but they understood circumstances in which both these things might be unavoidable. None of them looked upon themselves as killers, because the vampire they were about to dispatch was already dead, so they were just making sure it stayed in the grave. Still, one question preyed upon them all. Could they slay this abomination if it appeared as a little girl rather than a bat?

What lies before us and what lies behind us are small matters compared to what lies within us. And when we bring what is within out into the world, miracles can happen. This was what made Lynton such a formidable foe of evil. She simply had that special quality that elevated her above the norm, a quality that did not eliminate fear, but allowed her to rise above it in the quest for justice. She was the old time sheriff who strode out into the street at high noon to make a stand for justice against overwhelming odds. She was the lone person who refused to fall for demagoguery while millions were bowing in supplication. She was the monkey wrench in the machinery of complacency. She was the woman who knew that any fool can make a rule and another fool will follow it without question. She was no fool!

She gathered herself for battle. Her limbs relaxed, her countenance grew, her determination slowly inched across her face. All there marvelled at her wilful transformation into a valiant warrior ready for the coming carnage. She was more beautiful and more powerful than any one of them there had ever seen her. She was carrying an invisible sword of justice that was going to slice through the evil that had, for too long, brought a torrent of misery on those who were easy prey.

She was almost smiling in anticipation, while she was weeping for those who had been victims. Like a youthful hermit, beauteous in a wilderness, she moved quietly with a vision of the woe she was about to deliver to evil. It was easy to see within her a rising cauldron of serious intent, as if the bell of justice was wringing in her head. So let it knell!

Even the light of the moon slowly and methodically waned. The sounds of the forest became muffled, as if the intrepid Dhampyr pursuers were underwater. Aside from the beat of Lynton's heart, no muscle moved as she surveyed the scene while pounding inside her was a rhythm of determination for her coming battle against the force of evil that had been judge, jury and executioner for at least four hundred people.

The air was still through mist and cloud as Lynton overcame with dedication to the cause any dread for what must be done. She took a deep breath and prepared to speak. "Be assured what must be done is deplorable to me, but this thing, this evil is not a child, not a bat, but it is a devil the likes of which you have never seen before. It was sired through Annabel by the most evil incarnation known to mankind, an evil being that would shame even Satan. She was fathered by Ambrogio, the name itself implying the very essence of evil. I tell each of you that it is best that I enter the lair alone, because I have dealt with this type evil before. If we go in together, our affinity for each other may cause foolish actions that could lead to disaster."

Wilton, his voice rising in near anger, said "I will not permit it. I am here for vengeance and to find my wife's remains. You cannot deny me. You cannot!"

It was then that Lynton looked at her sextant with the precise coordinates and replied with determination, "We have no time to argue. All of you do as you will, but I must penetrate the liar now before Lizzie flies again. Because if she flies again, she flies in pursuit of blood."

Angus said, the cold evening air infecting his throat and lungs as he inhaled deeper and faster, "jumping into that liar is not at all smart. Still, my heart beats frantically in this situation for all or nothing. Fail and my whole body will pay the price, run and the physical damage is limited mostly to my shins and knees, but the damage to my psyche for being a coward would be incalculable. Let's go!"

Lynton had no time to try and convince them of the danger they were about to face, because time was of the essence. She headed toward the dense thicket before them with the sextant and her bag of Dhampyr fighting paraphernalia in hand. All of them wilfully followed her.

Through a thicket so dense that they began to scratch themselves and bleed, they trudged ever forward with determination until they came into a clearing. Then, they saw in the distance a dark shadow standing before the entrance to a cave, the very shadow all of them knew had been the harbinger of coming calamity so many times. Derek had the urge to rush the figure that had appeared the night his mother disappeared, but Lynton reached over and touched him gently as if to urge restraint. His respect for her kept him perfectly still by her side.

The dark figure made a waving motion with its right hand and stopping motion with the left, as if to say danger waited if they entered. It was then that Lynton's assumptions of its benign nature were solidified.

The dark figure pointed at the arbutus tree to Lynton's left. She walked over and lodged between two huge branches was a metal box. She tried to pull it out, but years of being there had made the tree grow around it and she was simply too weak. Derek came to her aid and with great effort removed it and handed it to Lynton. She opened it and took out a very old paper and unfurled it. She began to read aloud: "To anyone who might find this, I hereby put pen to paper so that the truth of what is about to happen can be told. My daughter was kidnapped by her biological father, a vampire that goes by the name Blackie Redwood, but truth be known he is Ambrogio, the vilest beast ever known to mankind. His aim is to turn her into a minion as evil as is he. I know the only way out for her is death from a wooden stake through her heart. As a loving father, I shall deliver that blow to her with remorse, but also with the knowledge that it is the only way to save both her and the world great pain. After this act, I shall then kill myself, for without my daughter there is no reason to live."

So there before them stood the spirit of Dark Malcolm, a kind ghost that had sacrificed his own life for the love of a daughter who was not even his biological child. He truly understood love was not predicated on DNA, but on what is in the heart.

One could sense the intensity of his sadness as he stared at them with those dark, penetrating fiery red eyes that were filled with misery that had been endured all those years, as he had neither the power to end his own anguish nor the despair of his beloved daughter. He had failed by stabbing her with a wooden stake and missing the heart by probably a few centimetres. For over one hundred years he had endured the pain of watching the one he loved commit vile acts to maintain life, a life that was a living hell, a complete denial of what waited for all those of us called humans – eternal rest wrapped in the peaceful cloak of death. The ghost before them was no more than a chill in the air, a shimmer of mist, a diffusion of darkness.

The rising dampness caused a mist to form and Dark Malcolm became slightly out of focus, like a poorly taken photograph. It was then that what appeared to be a bat flew out of the cave and morphed into a child that methodically strode from behind Malcolm as it slowly congealed into a form with brilliant red, fiery, evil-looking eyes, a pasty white skin and the smile of a determined predator. Her clothes were old and tattered, and the white dress had a huge blood stain on it, a stain caused by sucking blood from animals, and now she needed human blood and there before her was a feast of humans, a veritable banquet of the elixir that made her whole! For a moment all was silent, but then she morphed back into a bat-like figure, crouched and leaped up to soar skyward. All instantly froze as Dark Malcolm motioned toward the cave, making them realize that all those appearances by Dark Malcolm over the years was to try and warn the victims that had been picked by his daughter for nourishment. He had tried so very hard to give them a warning.

Who thundering comes as if on a black steed,
With slackened bit and hoof of speed?
Beneath the clattering iron's sound
The caverned echoes wake around.

In lash for lash, and bound for bound;
The foam that streaks the courser's side
Seems gathered from the ocean-tide,
As though weary waves are sunk to rest.

But does hope have a trace?
What time shall strengthen, not efface?
Though young and pale, that sallow front
Is scathed by fiery passion's brunt.

Lynton and the Ladysmith Phantom

Though bent on earth by your evil eye,
Meteor-like thou glidest by.
Right well they view and deem thee one,
Who the non-brave would shun.

All there stood in awe at Lynton's pride,
As she would fight or die.
The charge was coming now,
But before evil Lynton would never bow.

They all hurriedly followed Dark Malcolm into the cave as the bat-like figure fluttered about the sky outside agitatedly streaking back and forth in front of the moon, plotting her attack on those who had defiled her liar of evil.

Once inside, the hideousness was numbing as they moved toward the back of the cave. There, between a crevice on the left and an abyss on the right were discarded bodies and skeletons of all the victims, both human and animals, as a result of Lizzie's insatiable appetite for blood all those years.

Dark Malcolm pointed towards a crevice to the left, which was obviously a way out to safety. He then softly patted his heart and again pointed to the crevice as if to say, "go and survive the evil that is about to come your way."

Lynton vehemently shook her head while pointing down to her black bag that she had placed on the ground. She took out an iron stake and held it up. Then she removed a bone saw that would be used to sever the head. The ghost's emotions were elevating to the point that one could sense the heartache that Dark Malcolm faced, but it was heartache that this spirit which had been denied the comfort of the grave craved for himself and his daughter. He stood staring with heavy lidded eyes and a slack mouth at the instruments that would be used to finally end his daughter's hideous existence.

Suddenly, a black bat streaked overhead in the cave, landing a few feet from Lynton. The bat morphed into a girl with a demeanour that accentuated a skeletal look and in her gaze at Lynton were daggers of malevolent intentions. Lynton's mind was temporarily robbed of emotion, as instead of running or screaming she stood more still than a mossy statue in the heart of a graveyard and just as cold and determined, while her companions were shivering in fear of Lizzie.

Lizzie beckoned at Lynton with fingers that rapidly faded to only a suggestion of form. She became more solid again, but this time her skin bore many silver scars, thick and jagged. Although Lizzie was not capable of words, Lynton could sense what she was thinking: "When you come to this place I shall have you. When you come with your divine soul shining in your eyes, I will snatch it away. I will overpower whatever strength you have and trap it in a cage of evil. I will own you, keep you, bring you pain. I have been banished to hunt blood for eternity, and I must have it at all costs. Fight me and I will wear you down, appease me and I will torture you for failing to give me the glory of my hunt. I'm not anything you can relate to from fiction. There is no way to make me your friend, only your master. I shall make you enjoy the rapture of my dark ways, the ways of power. The best you can hope for is that I may take pity on you and let you enjoy the slow death that comes from gradual nourishment I will take slowly from you rather than taking it all at once. The succulent ecstasy that I will enjoy from the leeching I give you will make you float into a state of oblivion as you realize the joy you bring me, your master."

Lizzie ran toward Lynton so fast that she appeared to be no more than a fleeting silhouette and she made no sound at all. Lizzie was whiter than snow.

Lynton and the Ladysmith Phantom

The iron dagger was in Lynton's hand. She was up on her toes, ready to strike. Lizzie saw the dagger and instantly realized its purpose. She slammed to a stop, her fiery red eyes blazing with a shocked stare at the instrument that could fell her. The confrontation was stymied.

Lynton's breath came in small spurts, hot and nervous, but determined. At her side, slender dark fingers curled into a sweaty hold on the iron dagger, while she raised herself on the front of her feet swinging forward as if prepared to ram her tormentor. Behind her, she could hear the wailing howls of Wilton Manly who had found a skeleton that still had a locket he had given his wife around its neck. He was holding the skeleton in his shaking arms, as if expecting it to somehow respond to his affection. His son, desperately trying to console him, wrapped his arms sympathetically around his father, while Angus, Dina and Sue stood in awe at the confrontation between Lynton and Lizzie, waiting for any word from Lynton for assistance. They waited. They waited and waited with bated breath.

It appeared panic might be setting in on Lizzie, as she realize she was up against a formidable foe. The ledge upon which Lynton suddenly realized she was standing was as wide as a single foot and with all the grip of black ice. It went right around to the back of the cave, and most certainly was treacherous to walk on, never to take even the weight of a child, and Lynton was no child. She took a look down. She glanced around the cave, her eyes searching for somewhere, anywhere that might allow her an escape to more favourable ground and a better chance of confronting the evil before her. She looked down again. One wrong move and she wasn't going to get the chance to hear Wayne admonish her for being careless and disobeying his orders not to get involved in any dangerous adventures.

Lynton actually began to look at Lizzie with pity, remembering something a Sunday School teacher once told her about Jesus never personally promising but one person a place with him in Paradise - not Peter, not Paul, not any of his disciples. No, he promised that to a convicted thief being executed alongside him.

Lynton suddenly spoke with sympathy for a girl who through the merging of a vampire and a human had been born into a life of misery. "I, unfortunately, cannot just kill you, I must separate your head from your body and put the two parts in separate pits and put shovels of dirt in your mouth until it is full of muck. I am forced to hear the suffocation of your cries. I want you to know I take no glory, no solace at all from what must be done. I think you are sorry for the evil you have been compelled to commit through no fault of your own, but being sorry will not save the victims that await your wrath in the future. You have been forced to take the beauty of life and devour it with evil."

The dead cannot breathe, but Lynton could have sworn that she saw Lizzie's chest rising and falling in anticipation of the coming charge. The battle was about to rage!

Lizzie's fanged teeth glistened in the darkness. Her fiery red eyes were wide and unblinking as they stared daggers of hate. She ran a bony-hand through her dark hair, as thin lips turned upwards into a sinister smile. She was like a raging bull with a bright red cape before it, preparing to charge.

Dark Malcolm had stood by with the same pain he had endured for so many years, and now he was determined to make a stand against the daughter he loved, a stand for her own good, a stand against the eternity of damnable acts she had committed and would have to commit in the future to survive. As he moved with gentle ease toward her, the pain of love wracked his body.

Lizzie's demeanour calmed and her fanged teeth disappeared into a quivering mouth as tears filled her fiery red eyes, flowing generously down her cheeks. She fell willingly into her father's embrace as he knelt down cradling her in his arms. She looked up at him pleadingly, asking for an end to all the years of pain as the offspring of the evil vampire, Ambrogio. She then turned her head toward Lynton, who now also had tears in her eyes as well. She was actually pleading with the dynamic dynamo to ease her pain, to end the years she had endured the unendurable. Lynton offered her the salvation for which she longed.

The shadow cried, and while he pressed

Lynton and the Ladysmith Phantom

His stepdaughter to his breast,
Mighty, mighty Lynton espies,
As their hope for salvation in her lies.
She gave such a nod to the same,
As might beseem so bright a dame!

Truth can be poisoned with a shove,
But here and now hope came.
And constancy lived in realms above;
And no longer would love be in vain;
And to be wroth with one we love
Doth work like madness in the brain.

The touch, the sight, had passed away,
And in its stead that vision blest
Which comforted Lizzie after rest,
While in her father's arms she lay,
As if he had put a rapture in her breast,
And on her lips she seemed to say, "All is O.K."

A little child, a limber elf,
Singing, dancing to itself,
A fairy thing with red round cheeks
That always finds, and forever seeks,
Makes such a vision to the sight
As fills a father's eyes with light.

And pleasures flow in so thick and fast
Upon Malcolm's heart that he at last
Must again express his love's excess
Without words of any bitterness.
Perhaps 'tis pretty to force together

Lynton and the Ladysmith Phantom

Thoughts all like each other.

To mutter with sadness a broken charm,
To dally with wrong that did so much harm.
Perhaps 'tis tender too and pretty
At each wild word to feel within
A sweet recoil of love and pity,
For surely a father's love is not a sin.

Lynton moved very slowly with great deliberateness and extreme gentleness toward the two, as her companions looked on in complete awe at her incredibly persistent resolve and extreme valour. Father and daughter did not waver as they awaited the end. Lynton drove the iron stake into Lizzie's heart, reached down and gently removed her from her father's arms as Lizzie belched up fluid and quivered as Lynton laid her on the ground.

Lynton reached into her bag and brought out the bone saw. With tears in her eyes, she looked over at Dark Malcolm. Continuing to kneel as if his beloved daughter was still in his arms, he lowered his head in acquiescence to what must be done, but he could not watch.

He loved the little girl so,
But for her sake he must let go.
He passed not of his name and race,
And left not a token or a trace,
Save what the father must not say
Who watched her dismembered that day.

Lynton and the Ladysmith Phantom

There are times when Lynton hates her overwhelming determination, times when she deplores the power she possesses to eradicate evil, times when she looks with dismay on the grit she manifests to chase demons that prey upon people's fears, times when she longs for a normal life free of the tenacity that will not allow her the luxury to walk away from trouble or turn her back on those suffering. This was one of those times, because beneath her was Lizzie awaiting the coup de grâce, almost pleading for Lynton to end her pain.

The saw tore into flesh, and blood gushed out from severed veins and arteries, splashing not only onto Lynton's clothes but on her face. She fought valiantly to keep from throwing up, as her companions turned their heads away in horror.

Once the task was completed, she looked tearfully at the severed head she now held by the hair in her right hand. The power of speech had long vanished from Lizzie's lips, but the eyes looked up at Lynton as if to say, "thank you for setting me free." Then they closed.

Lynton, in an almost whisper, said to her companions, "The task is done. You can all look now."

Angus asked, "What can we do?"

She replied, "You must bury the body as far away from here as possible. I will walk to the other side of the mountain and bury the head, placing the mouth full of dirt. We must never reveal what happened; only tell the authorities that we, while hiking, came upon this killing ground."

Still, there before them was the kneeling Dark Malcolm. He arose. He walked over to the abyss, looked back at Lynton with sorrowful eyes that seemed to, like his daughter's eyes, be saying "thank you for freeing me." He fell forward into the abyss, disappearing into a mist and Lynton walked out with her companions.

Angus said, "I'll go with you while the others bury the torso."

She replied, "It is better I do it alone, so no one knows the location of the head. I will meet you back at Sue's house, and then we will all get our story straight and go to the police."

The two parties separated, and as Angus and Derek carried the torso, Sue turned and watched Lynton as she disappeared over the crest of the mountain. She could not help but think of the line from Shakespeare: *The night is long that never finds the day.*

Epilogue
Mark of a Dhampyr

Laugh, and the world laughs with you;
Weep, and you weep alone;
For the sad old earth must borrow its mirth,
But has trouble enough of its own.
Sing and the hills will answer;
Sigh, and it is lost on the air;.
The echoes bound to a joyful sound,
But shrink from voicing care.

Rejoice, and men will seek you;
Grieve, and they turn and go.
They want full measure of all your pleasure,
But they do not need your woe.
Be glad, and your friends are many;

Lynton and the Ladysmith Phantom

Be sad, and you lose them all.
There are none to decline your nectared wine,
But alone you must drink life's gall.

Feast, and your halls are crowded;
Fast, and the world goes by.
Succeed and give, and it helps you live,
But no man can help you die.
There is room in the halls of pleasure
For a large and lordly train,
But one by one we must all file on
Through the narrow aisles of pain.

It has been said that time heals all wounds. The truth is that wounds will always remain. In time, the mind, protecting its need for sanity, covers those wounds with scar tissue and the pain does lessen. But it is never gone for those who have hearts that beat with the determined rhythm of love. Dark Malcolm knew the pain of love that had captured him in the throes of untold misery as he longed to bring the daughter he adored some peace. Finally, Lynton did that which he was unable to do.

Lynton took some solace in the fact that she had been able to end a reign of terror, but still she felt weariness that Lizzie had to suffer death twice in order to obtain release from misery that was not of her own making. She had been a victim just as much as those whose blood she had devoured in the search for sustenance. Was she any different than the callous corporate executives that devoured the very life out of people for the sake of greed? Their greed was for money; hers for blood, but unlike them, Lizzie had an excuse. They had none!

How many times in life do people beat on a wall trying to make it a door? We are all hemmed in by walls that make us slaves in a world where earning our daily bread, for most of us, occupies all our time, leaving little time for things that really matter. We are bombarded with pleas for us to buy, because buying things is supposed to bring that ever elusive happiness. True happiness does not lie in material things, but in the emotional depths of love that means we must be willing to embrace the sad that often comes with the happy. Dark Malcolm had more love than most people are capable of. His devotion to his daughter was so extraordinary that it continued long after his death.

So, two weeks later, as Lynton sat at Sue's house with her companions from the great adventure that freed two tormented souls, she looked at Wayne and Bruce, who had joined them, and realized that she was a recipient of the kind of love from Wayne that was shared between Lizzie and Dark Malcolm. She felt it every moment of every day from the husband who idolized her, worshipped and adored her. She felt the warmth of love from a man who had himself suffered great pain as a result of loving two other women who had betrayed him. She, too, had experienced the same pain when she caught her lover with another woman. Like her, Wayne was on the verge of giving up when she miraculously popped into his life one night when he saw her singing in a Vancouver nightclub. It was Wayne who told her as she lay in his arms on their wedding night, "I am so thankful for the pain I suffered, because if I had not suffered that pain I would have never found you."

Lynton's pensive nature was obvious, and Angus, assuming she was thinking about their incredible adventure and fighting back morose feelings as a result of what happened to so many victims, including Malcolm and Lizzie, said "Don't be sad Lynton; you did a deed almost no one else could have had the courage to do. You freed two tortured souls from unimaginable misery."

Smiling, Lynton replied with a poem:

I sit beside the fire and think
Of all that I have seen
Of meadows, flowers and butterflies
In summers that have been.

Of yellow leaves and gossamer
In autumns that were
Filled with morning mist and silver sun
And wind upon my hair.

I sit beside the fire and think
Of how the world will be
When winter comes without a spring
That I shall never see.

Lynton and the Ladysmith Phantom

For still there are so many things
That I have never seen.
In every wood in every spring
There is a different green.

I sit beside the fire and think
Of people long ago,
And people that will see a world
That I shall never know.

But all the while I sit and think
Of times there were before
I listened for returning feet
And voices at my door.

There were still many unanswered questions, and it was Sue who directed a pertinent question to Lynton who now seemed to be in a contemplative state, "There are so many unanswered questions still. For example, I truly wonder what my mother meant when she said, 'it has killed him.' Do you know what she meant?"

Seemingly coming out of her near trance, Lynton replied, "Only conjecture, of course, but I think she meant the Dhampyr had killed your father. Remember how your father saw the figure coming out of the forest? It was Lizzie. Remember how his face was almost obliterated? The shotgun blast was from Lizzie after she had feasted on his blood. She wanted to destroy obvious evidence of her deed. Your mother had been targeted, but so had your father. Dark Malcolm had probably tried to warn them both of impending doom, and the night your mother died it was Malcolm in that corner, trying to warn her again about Lizzie's intent to make your mother her next victim. Of course, your mother's death that night precluded Lizzie from feasting on her fresh blood."

Dina then asked, "What of the woman, the child and the dark figure on the ferry.

"Well, in my humble opinion, the woman and child on the ferry have absolutely nothing to do with Dark Malcolm, who was obviously the cloaked figure sitting across from you two. That mother and child were simply two ghosts from long ago. I did some research, and a woman and child who had attended the funeral of the mother's child by another marriage were on board the very first sailing of a B.C. Ferry's ship from Tsawwassen to Swartz Bay on June 15, 1960. On that voyage, the two disappeared, and it was assumed they had fallen overboard. My guess is the woman committed suicide and took her child with her when she jumped off the ship, unseen by anyone. They were ghosts. Now, why Dark Malcolm was there sitting across from you, I have no idea, except maybe it was another warning. That is a mystery I am afraid I have been unable to solve, unless there might have been some indication that Lizzie was going to target one of you as her victim."

"Lizzie's mother," asked Sue, "Lizzie actually sucked her own mother's blood in the forest that day when they were found?"

"Again, only conjecture," replied Lynton, "but my guess is yes, because she knew her mother aimed to destroy her, so why not satisfy her craving for blood and eliminate her at the same time. Hard to imagine a three year old, almost four, capable of murder, but stranger things have happened."

Derek asked, "Lizzie and Malcolm could not speak, but what of the whimpering?"

Smiling Lynton shrugged her shoulders and said, "Obviously I cannot answer every question you have, but perhaps ghosts are capable of crying if not speaking, and that is why scrawled in the sand was her plea for you to help her. Lizzie was actually not all bad; we found that out when she accepted her fate. No, when she embraced her fate!"

Sue then asked, "And what of the Ace of Spades? What did that mean in the dream?"

"That is the dark card, the card of evil. It was just a dream, but like many dreams it was a warning, a subconscious sensing that something bad was about to happen. No doubt her friend was taken by Lizzie as he stood at the door of her house with the ace of spades in his hand."

"So many people," offered Dina, "so many people who just disappeared and were forgotten, overlooked by the authorities."

Lynton said, "Once testing is done on all the remains from that infernal cave, I am sure so many victims long forgotten by the authorities will be identified – the boatman and his son, Harry

Stammer from the hotel and First Nations people who were dismissed as unworthy to be concerned about."

Sue then said, "And one final question that still mystifies me. What of the picture locked away in that room?"

"I have no idea where the picture came from, but it may have been done somehow, in someway by none other than Dark Malcolm as another one of his warnings. It depicted Lizzie as a child and as a bat. It also depicted Blackie Redwood, who was Ambrogio, and, of course, Dark Malcolm himself. I believe some things are best left alone. I suggest leaving the room sealed, and never letting that painting see the light of day. Your parents were wise to lock that abomination up and seal the room."

"It has been such a rollercoaster of emotions, such a mystifying journey into the macabre and such a terrifying realization for me that those of us who are not affluent seem to have less importance in this world. I am dumbfounded about how we can somehow be sure every person is valued and given the justice deserved. It appears that a lot of our efforts have been wasted, because no one really cares." said Derek.

Wayne, sitting quietly through all the discussion looked at Derek and said, "Don't get too discouraged. I have often been discouraged as a writer, because I believe I have something important to say, but so many of my books are complete flops. Yet, I try to always remember what Ernest Hemingway said, 'If your words only reach one person who is affected by them, then you are a successful writer.' My dear Aunt Willa Mae Cagle was my biggest and probably only fan in Asheboro, North Carolina where I grew up. She always used to look forward to my books, because she said that she found wisdom in my words, wisdom that offered insightful observations on the human condition. When she died a few years ago my motivation diminished, because I had lost my biggest fan, but that old saying that when one door closes another one opens is very apropos. A high school classmate of mine from that same town, Phyllis Strider Williams, got in touch with me just by chance after my aunt died. We had not talked in nearly fifty years. She relayed to me how much she enjoyed my books. Now when I begin a book, she provides my motivation. I want to write something she finds interesting. That is the story of life; we need inspiration from family, from friends, even from strangers. Doing things for ourselves is very poor motivation, but doing things for others is what gives our lives meaning. You have all done something kind. You will go unsung, unacknowledged, unhailed, unacclaimed and unrecognized, but you all know in your hearts that you brought peace to Dark Malcolm and Lizzie. You set two miserable souls lose from bondage."

Lynton looked at Wayne with thankfulness in her heart, because he had given her friends the pat on the back they so justly deserved.

Lynton and the Ladysmith Phantom

Wayne, Bruce and Lynton got up to leave, saying goodnight to all. Derek and Sue walked them to the door. Lynton gave Sue a goodnight hug, and in doing so she inadvertently dislodged Sue's ear ring. It fell to the floor and Sue bent over to pick it up, causing her straight, thin hair to slightly expose her upper scalp. Lynton remembered Sue's supposed dream of being in the forest and feeling pain in her neck. It was definitely not a dream. The flower on the floor had proven that. She had been bitten by Lizzie. Lynton shivered with fear. There, on her scalp was a red birthmark in the shape of a bat's right wing – the mark of a Dhampyr!

The End Or Is It

DON'T MISS
THESE LYNTON ADVENTURES

Lynton Curls Her Hair
Lynton Walks on Water
Lynton and the Vampire at Tagaytay Manor
Lynton Buys a Cell-Phone and Hears the Voice of Doom
Lynton Viñas and Beowulf Perez in the Taal Inferno*
Lynton and the Ghosts in the Mansion on Balete Drive
Lynton Viñas: Shadow in the Darkness
Lynton's South African Adventure
Lynton, the Karoo Vampire and the Jewels of Omar Bin Abi
Lynton and the Haunting of the HMS Wind Dancer
Lynton and the Stellenbosch Terror
Lynton and the Cape Town Ghost
Pursuit*
Lynton and Chablis in the Room of Doom*

*recommended for age 16 and above only

J. Wayne Frye